THE ALICE DIARIES

Kathleen Ryder

DECEMBER

Monday 9 December

Dear Diary,

I spent the better part of today holding my breath. I sometimes feel that I never exhale, not really, not fully. There was another official-looking envelope in the mail today, my traitorous fingers shook trying to open it, tearing at the edge, roughly, anxiously. I am conflicted, between a yearning to know what is inside, and the fear of finding out. I pulled the letter out, a standard trifold printed on white typing paper, and skimmed the page quickly. My heart sank as the news registered. It's okay, it wasn't from the bank, we're safe, Ronnie and I are not going to be homeless just yet. It was another impersonal rejection letter, the fourth one I have had this week alone. I folded it in half and quickly stuffed it inside my pocket, hoping against hope that no one saw me do it, I just did not want any questions today, I just could not face them, not today. I honestly do not understand how it can be so hard to find a job in Alice Springs. It's not as if I am completely unskilled, I have administration experience, years and years of demoralising administration experience. I'm not even that fussy, to be honest, I don't mind working as a checkout operator at a supermarket, or...Actually, apart from administration or checkout operator, I don't have skills in anything else. Alice Springs is a tourist town; they want baristas and tour guides and pretty young things who can flirt with customers. They don't want someone like me, a middle-aged, overweight, outspoken single mum with excess baggage and bi-racial parentage. I'm not stupid, I know what they mean when they say they had more suitable candidates, they mean they had whiter candidates. The funny thing is, I don't even know why I am so upset, I didn't even want the job, not really, I only applied because I loathe my current job, the money was decent, and it was a position that I know I can do. Not that that means much, I dare say anyone can do admin if they choose to. I don't know why I even bother looking for work anymore, I am so tired of always being looked over, of being on everyone's "don't touch" list. It is just so very hard. All I want to do is make a better life for Ronnie, for him to have everything that I never had as a child, things that other people take for granted, like three meals a day, a good school, a safe place to live. He worries so much about me, more than a nine-year-old should worry, that is for sure. He should be full of the innocence of youth, this precious child of mine, he should be giddy and carefree, instead of worried and anxious for me. I hate that he is turning into me. My entire childhood was filled with stress and worry, of empty bellies and pretending I was fine. On days like today I feel much older than my nearly thirty-five years. I don't think I am depressed, but then again, how would I know? Life is hard, it always has been, it always will be. The only difference is that I am now so very tired of the effort of trying to live.

Alice

Monday 16 December

Dear Diary,

The end of another year, I can't even begin to tell you how much I both look forward to, and dread, this time of the year. Time is fast running out for me, statistically speaking. A bi-racial female, living in the isolated outback, yeesh! It's a wonder I'm not already dead! I joke about it, my mortality, because the truth is, it scares me. This fragile life we have, struggling to scratch out some kind of existence, constantly lying to ourselves about our own happiness. It is exhausting! I look at my son, and I know true fear. I am scared for him, for his future. People can be so very cruel to those who are seen as different, and they are very quick to pass judgement. I wish I could give him a different version of life. I always dreamt of a different life when I was younger, even when dreaming wasn't encouraged, not for someone like me in any case. They weren't unkind, the teachers, I realise that now, they were simply being realistic, even though each rebuttal, each rejection, chipped away at my dreams – chip, chip, chip – until I simply stopped dreaming. What was the point? The teachers were right to look at me with pity in their eyes, they were right to stamp out my dreams. After all, what right did I have to dream? A shy girl with an abusive half Indigenous father and an emotionally vacant English mother. I was lucky to even be allowed to attend primary school, at least that is what I overheard the teachers saying one day, and maybe they were right, a look at my year one school photo clearly shows a very white class, the early eighties were not big on multiculturalism. I can still remember the moment I stood up in class on the last day of term two and made my announcement. The teacher wanted everyone to tell her what they wanted to be when they grew up, and I couldn't wait! We had heard all the usual answers of teacher, firefighter, dancer and so on, and now it was my turn. I stood quickly, knocking my chair over in haste. Sucking in a deep breath, I told everyone that when I grew up, I wanted to be happy! There was the briefest moment of stunned silence, followed by laughter. The class thought I was being funny, the teacher told me not to be silly, that I had to choose something 'proper'. It's funny how life turns out. All of my dreams dropped along the wayside, empty memories of a girl desperate to belong. That shy girl became an adult, protectively aloof, still desperate to belong. Even after everything, I still cling to some distant hope that my most coveted dream will come true, that maybe one day I will learn what complete happiness is, for me and my son. Or at the very least, that I will learn to accept life as it is, instead of always chasing what should have been, what I wanted it to be. In my darker moments, I start to wonder if I even know what it is to be happy. Maybe I am incapable of feeling happy? Maybe I have some chemical imbalance that predetermines me to be unhappy? Even as I write that, I know it is not true. Dead people can't feel anything, and I have been dead for a long time, twenty-eight years to be exact. My soul was fractured when I was seven, and slowly, so very slowly over the years, despair has seeped in, eroding my soul with rust from the inside out. I don't know who I am anymore, perhaps I never did? How can I know myself, my true self, when my psyche was changed inexplicitly? I didn't see it happening, wasn't aware of how darkly neurotic I was becoming, until recently. Now that I know, I am not sure how to fix it.

Alice

Tuesday 31 December

Dear Diary,

Having decided not to think about my neurotic soul or my current state of unhappiness, I have, of course, obsessed over nothing else these past couple of weeks. Here is what I know:

1. I want to change; I want to be abundantly happy.

2. I want to set a deadline; I don't want to drag it out unnecessarily. I am giving myself twelve months, to chase what it is I want.

This time next year, if nothing has changed, I will accept the stereotypical fate society has forced upon me and hope for a better outcome for Ronnie.

I Will Not...

- Eat when feeling sad, anxious, worried, lonely or down in the dumps.

- Waste any more money buying evening gowns, as pointless since have no one to wear it for.

- Get annoyed with interfering yet (supposedly) well-meaning relatives.

- Wander around the house in only a tee shirt and underwear and will instead try to dress as a perfect mother should.

- Sulk about current life situation, but rather try to change in productive and helpful ways.

- Fall for men who are unavailable, gay, mentally unstable, racist, or who are otherwise not interested in me.

- Obsess (too much) over past mistakes.

- Try to fill my emotional needs by buying things
- Keep fantasising about Caleb as it is pathetic to be so hung up on a guy who has absolutely zero interest in me.

I Will...

- Learn to program the microwave clock.
- Lose 50 kilos and tighten my tuck shop arms.
- Reduce my swearing to an acceptable level.
- Eat more vegetables, especially green ones, regardless of how revolting they taste.
- Limit myself to one small treat each week.
- Clear out all the clothes that don't fit.
- Improve career prospects by doing a course.
- Be assertive and more confident.
- Stop apologising for who I am.

- Watch socially popular television shows so will have something to talk about at work.

- Watch the news every day for the same reason.

- Limit myself to ten minutes per day on any social media platform.

- Stop making dream wedding boards on Pinterest, as pointless as not likely to be getting married.

- Don't spend any money unless it is absolutely essential.

Alice

JANUARY

Wednesday 1 January

Dear Diary,

Hmm, not the most splendid start to the new year if I am totally honest! It has only just begun and already I am so very weary. My mother had another one of her epic moods today, all because Ronnie didn't want to play chess with her. She went on and on about how no one ever wants to do anything with her, they just sit around and ignore her. Seriously?! Toddler much?! We are so used to her moods now, that we just tune her out, but it is still exhausting, having to constantly be on high alert in your own home, lest you say the wrong thing to trigger her today. Honestly, I wish she didn't live with me, I wish I wasn't such a pushover that I allowed her to live with me, to remain living with me even after Ronnie and I moved house, moved states. Every time I even start to broach the subject of her perhaps moving out, of starting her own life somewhere, she plays the emotional blackmail card. She has nowhere else to go. She'll have to live in her car. She can't afford to. Woe, woe, woe. So, I let her stay, because it is true. She has nowhere else to go. She has no friends, all her family have disowned her years ago, her own daughter included. I am a pushover and she knows it, she uses it, me, to her advantage, and I am too scared of her to stand up for myself. It has been this way my entire life, pandering to her, trying to keep on her good side, placating her. It is incredibly exhausting! As I am rostered off work tomorrow, I decided it would be fun to try and stay up with Ronnie to welcome in the new year. Unfortunately, a dinner of homemade hamburgers with the lot, combined with the cinema lighting Ronnie insists on watching television by, meant we both dozed off sometime around 10 o'clock in the evening, watching reruns of our favourite comedy. OMG, the lead actor is some yummy eye candy, definitely fantasy inducing! I woke up wishing things were different. Wishing I had money, wishing I had a licence, wishing I had a car, wishing I was married, wishing I could get rid of my mother, wishing I had friends, wishing I was happy. Wishing, wishing, wishing. Mostly I woke up wishing that I knew how to make things different, better. I hate when I wake up distressed, it is so disorientating. Despite the dodgy start, this year is going to be My Year, I just know it! I am going to shed this old life of mine and emerge into my new (better) life thinner, fitter, and full of unshakeable confidence. Starting tomorrow.

Alice

Friday 3 January

Dear Diary,

Oh my gosh, I am so over this year already and it has only just started! I made the mistake of going down to the supermarket today to pick up a couple of things.

Actually, the mistake wasn't so much going there, as it was in taking my mother along with me! Not that I have much choice though, she has made sure of that over the years. The supermarket was, as usual, dingy and chaotic. Why is it that they never have any manned checkouts open? I mean seriously! Urgh, anyway, I finally got through the self-service checkout with my trolley full of groceries (isn't it funny how three things you need can turn into twenty-nine bags of foodstuffs that you are supposed to be swearing off), and was commenting to mother about how awful the supermarket is, and just why this will be the absolute last time that I ever step foot into the store again, when she turned to me and screamed at the top of her lungs, "shut the feck up!" Obviously, she didn't say "feck", she used the non-censored word, but I am trying not to swear this year. In any case, I was so humiliated, my face felt as if it were on fire, and all the other nearby customers all turned around and looked at us, at me. I was beyond mortified. I don't understand why she is so hateful towards me; I think sometimes that she must have some kind of mental illness, she runs so very hot and cold. Of course, she refuses to listen whenever I bring up the possibility of her actually seeing a doctor to have any type of assessment conducted. On top of which, I feel like death warmed up, I hope that I am not coming down with anything. In any case, dealing with her moods again made for a very tiring day and I am having an early night with Ronnie in front of the television. Tomorrow I will try to go for a walk.

Alice

Saturday 4 January

Dear Diary,

I am feeling so ill today, I woke up with such a nasty sore throat, it feels almost like it has pus on the sides, which is not only uncomfortable but also really gross to think about. I really hope that I am not getting sick, I hate being sick, not because of the pain or anything like that, but rather because when I get sick, I get very depressed. It is as if the act of being sick opens up my mind to all of the secrets I keep there, the poisonous tendrils that usually only manage to escape in the middle of the night, tormenting me through dreams and insomnia. When I am sick, the barricades that I have erected in order to protect me, to hide me, are weakened, and all of the poison seeps out. Of course, the other is also true. With the door slightly ajar, all of the nasty abuse I endure while sick manages to get into my mind, my soul, and acts as new fuel for my already overwhelmed brain. Being sick, for me, goes hand in hand with being depressed and suicidal. Apart from all of that, one of the ladies I work with, well past retirement age, likes to consider herself as the senior administrative officer, and she does not like it if anyone needs to take a day off due to being sick, although it does give her something new to whinge and gloat about. Which is pretty ironic considering that she herself is seldom on time, and somehow manages to get nearly every Friday off work, convenient seeing as how she is the one who does up the rosters! I have been working in that role for two years now, yet she still refers to me as 'the girl who stole my job'. She is only on a contract, and the job I initially applied for was her job, advertised as a permanent role. I was successful, she was not. She was then offered another contract position so that she could remain on staff. She has never gotten over it, is convinced that I only got the position because I am bi-racial. She makes snide remarks about 'your land' and even went as far as to tell me that 'you are not like other mixed-race people I have worked with; you seem to enjoy working and actually show up, which is a nice change'. I know she is waiting for me to call in sick, so out of sheer determination, I have managed to work through any sickness I have had so far. I always have to watch what I say while I am around her, it is so stressful. Honestly, it makes for such a toxic work environment. I am thinking that this first week of the year is a write-off, I doubt that I will be up to walking tomorrow. Or even moving off the couch for that matter. I guess it will give me an excuse to binge-watch something on TV before my free trial runs out. I don't think I shall keep the subscription past the trial stage, it is way overpriced for the shows they have on offer, and I am not home enough to get any real value from it. Besides, I promised myself that I would watch popular shows this year, the type of shows that everyone else at work is watching, and the shows that I binge watch are not what one would call popular, rather reruns of shows from the nineties. Better stick to free to air channels so that I can at least pretend to know what people are talking about at work, I hate feeling like such an outsider. I already have a hard enough time trying to fit in as it is, even after all of this time, you would think that I would get used to it, but I never have.

Alice

Sunday 5 January

Dear Diary,

It is official, I am definitely sick. I woke up this morning with a nasty temperature, the same pus-filled throat as yesterday, and some dreadfully swollen glands. I am in so much pain I can barely speak, let alone be heard. It took me nearly five minutes to explain to work just who was actually calling them, and why. they were not very impressed that I was taking today off work, but seriously, I work on a god damn switchboard, if they couldn't hear me on the phone, what makes them think that anyone else will be able to understand me, never mind the strain that it would put on my voice box. Honestly, the management staff I work with are such selfish individuals. I am lucky that I have tomorrow rostered off work, I really cannot afford to be taking time off, I just get way too much slack for it afterwards. I booked in to see the doctor tomorrow, they are actually open seven days, but they only bulk bill on weekdays, and there is no way that I can afford to pay to see someone on the weekend. Actually, that's not entirely true. I can afford to; I just refuse to. Paying the higher fee on the weekend would mean that I have less to spend on groceries this fortnight, and there is no way that Ronnie will ever go hungry, not while I have breath in my body. Besides, why pay more than I have to? There is an after-hours doctor clinic at the hospital, that I can access for free as a single mum on a low income, but having used it one before, I now refuse to go back there. Firstly, I don't think the doctor that mans it is very professional, he went to look in my throat without first washing his hands or wearing gloves! I don't think so! And secondly, just because I am poor doesn't mean that I can't afford to pay for a doctor of my choice. No matter how poor I am, I should still be able to see a doctor of my choosing, not one that has been assigned to a free clinic in order to gain community experience. Anyway, it is embarrassing, going into the free clinic. I don't need charity, I'm not destitute, not yet anyway. I slept for most of the day, Ronnie sat next to me and watched some of his favourite shows on the television. He gets so worried when I am sick, try as I might, I struggle to reassure him that everything will be okay. I know better than anyone that no one can keep a promise like that! My mother pottered around, making as much noise as humanly possible, hoping, I suspect, that I would ask her what she was doing. I resisted the urge.

Alice

Monday 6 January

Dear Diary,

The doctor says that I have a case of strep throat and bronchitis, what joy. I have a crap tonne of medications to take, including a steroid one for my lungs, which may make it harder to sleep. Ha, that is laughable! If I ever slept more than five hours a night people would think I had died! I just wish I had some kind of backup system or tribe of people around me who could lend a hand when I was sick. It is hard to be there for Ronnie when I feel like this. Bless him, he tries so hard to help out, bringing me blankets and tissues and glasses of water; but there is no way he can do the big things, like get dinner sorted, or clean the house, not that I would ever ask or expect him to. Good grief, I am not my mother! Speaking of her, she has stayed in her room for most of the day, ignoring everyone. It has been surprisingly peaceful. Still, days like this, when I feel so ill, I wish I had a large family, or a normal family, you know, one that cares for each other. It is hard to be so alone. I can mask it, mostly. It is easy enough to do during the day, or when Ronnie is around. If I just keep busy enough, it doesn't matter if the phone rings or not, as I won't have time to talk anyway. The phone never rings. Sometimes I wonder what it must be like to have a friend. Is it as nice as the movies would have you believe? Is there laughter and chatting and confidences being kept? Are there in-jokes and random lunch dates and always being there for each other? Or is it all a lie perpetuated by Hollywood? Either way, I just wish that I knew.

Alice

Tuesday 7 January

Dear Diary,

I spent most of the day in bed, watching television and napping. If I wasn't feeling so ill, it would have been a perfect day! I know that when I get sick, I tend to get depressed, so I am trying to think positively today. I didn't check social media once today, I feel so liberated, and more than a bit relieved. It is hard to keep seeing everyone's happy and successful lives. I don't know why I keep looking at it, to be honest, it only makes me irritated, and more than a little bit jealous. It is only natural, I suppose, to want what everyone else has. Nice furniture, yummy food, fancy overseas holidays. The problem is, when you have no hope of ever having those things, comparison really is the thief of joy. I want to teach Ronnie to be happy with what he has, not because it is all he can ever hope of having, but rather because what he already has is a blessing in his life, and a darn sight more than a lot of people already have. I want to try and teach that to myself as well! My mother attempted to start another fight with me, but I was having none of it! She started complaining about how she has to drive me into town to see the doctor, as I don't have a driving licence, blah, blah, blah. Whose fault is that? I simply reminded her that she was the one who refused to teach me how to drive, that it was her who had refused to contribute financially to me having driving lessons. Both of these things would have been perfectly fine, except for the fact that she then paid for both of my younger siblings to have their driving lessons, as well as taking them out for additional lessons. She would not even take me to go and sit for my learner's test, I had to walk to the train station in the next suburb, get the train and then a bus into the city, and sit the test. I was lucky to have found a copy of the road user's manual at the local library or I would not have even been able to study the road rules before sitting the test. My sister and brother were given brand new copies that mother purchased at the newsagent. When questioned as to the obvious double standards, she merely said that they were safer drivers than me. Um, how would she know?! When I eventually had enough money to be able to pay for driving lessons, she refused to watch Ronnie for me, telling me that Ronnie was not her child, so why should she watch him. I couldn't afford to pay for a babysitter and pay for a driving instructor, and without a sitter for Ronnie, I was unable to have lessons. There is no doubt in my mind as to why she really refused to enable me to have driving lessons. She enjoys being controlling and manipulative. She likes to keep me on a tight leash, it is the only way that she can perpetuate her constant abuse against me, by keeping me essentially trapped and dependent upon her. I despise her so much; I honestly cannot wait for her to die. Sometimes I think that the only way I shall ever be happy, the only chance I really have of ever having a real life, will be when she dies. I wish that I could talk to someone about it, but who the hell would listen? Everyone thinks that I am so very *lucky* to have my mother living with me, they imagine that she does all sorts of wonderful mother type things to help me out. I can't tell anyone the truth, how could I? She is so very clever at hiding her true self, at being congenial whenever there are other people around. It is only when we are alone that she confesses that she comes into my room at night, that I have no idea how many times she has watched me sleep, just thinking about stabbing me to death. Charming! Who would believe me? Parents don't abuse their adult children, how ridiculous does that sound? No, who would I tell? So, I suffer in silence, each day dying a little bit more on the inside, no longer able to remember a time when I was happy, if at all. There are only two things that keep me tied to this earth: Ronnie, and three little words, maybe one day...

Alice

Wednesday 8 January

Dear Diary,

I am feeling so very drained and tired tonight. I ended up going back to the doctor today, I was so breathless last night that I thought that I would have to go up to the hospital. He ran some tests, and it came back positive for whooping cough. Again. I most likely caught it from the hospital in the first place I imagine, that place is a cesspool of disease and germs. On New Year's Eve 1999, when everyone was paranoid about the Y2K virus, I was battling a different kind of virus, whooping cough. I was at home, feeling unwell, when I suddenly couldn't breathe. I headed up to the hospital, and the waiting room was chaos! Full of interesting characters, including a man with a placard declaring the world is about to end, and honestly, at that moment, I thought it actually would. Initially, the doctors thought I had legionnaires disease, along with the man in the cubicle next to mine, but tests later revealed it to be whooping cough. Thank goodness! Saved me a lot of embarrassment, as the only place I had been visiting that had had air conditioning, was the local sports club to play Keno! The treatment was six months of steroids, and now my left lung has a capacity thirty percent lower than my right lung. Hopefully, this bout won't last for as long and I will bounce back a lot quicker. I didn't sleep well last night; I wish I could find some way out of this life I have found myself in. I keep thinking up ways of leaving with Ronnie, of being able to escape, but every plan I come up with has so many drawbacks they are not really feasible. My mother has cost me so much, I don't think she even knows. Or if she does, she makes no mention of it and certainly doesn't seem to care either way!

Alice

Thursday 9 January

Dear Diary,

Oh my god, I woke up today with the most insanely itchy vagina! I'm not talking about a fleeting itch that can be cured with a quick scratch through my underwear. Oh no, I am talking about a full-blown, what the actual feck, mother of all itches. I feel like the only thing that will assuage this itch is to attack it with one of those really harsh spikey hairbrushes, or maybe a wire brush, neither of which I intend to do! I am in so much agony from this unrelenting itch, I can barely concentrate on anything else. Naturally, I used the internet to look up my symptoms, as you do in this day and age, and I discovered that the medication I am on for my whooping cough has a very common side effect of causing thrush, or in other words, a super insanely itchy vagina! On the plus side, the itch should disappear in three to five days. If not, I should seek medical advice. Let's hope it goes away, there is no way on Earth I would ever see a doctor for this! God, how embarrassing! My internet search suggested that live cultures can help ease the itch, but even if I had yoghurt in the house, there is no way I would scoop it onto my vagina, how squidgy would that be, totally gross. So, I tried cheese instead. In sheer desperation, I hacked off a chunk of cheese and just wore it in my undies all morning, although to be honest, that was also super gross! It turns out that my body heat is pretty high, and the cheese wilted pretty quickly. Still, desperate times call for desperate measures and all that. Hopefully, tomorrow will be better and I shall have some relief.

Alice

Friday 10 January

Dear Diary,

Still insanely itchy! To be honest, I am not sure how much more I can endure before I crumble and go to see a doctor. I am in so much pain from the itching, I haven't been able to concentrate on anything else at all. I literally sat here all day, keeping my legs as tightly shut as possible, as if by pressing them together I can somehow stop the itch. I tried pain relief, hot and cold packs, and still, the itch persists. I watched a movie on subscription television with Ronnie tonight, about an obese woman with an active, if not humiliating, sex life, deciding to get fit and run a marathon. To be honest it wasn't anything like I was expecting it to be. I cried, as I do with pretty much any movie these days. It was like watching myself, only without the blow jobs. Or indeed the sex at all. It was heartbreakingly sad, and I haven't stopped thinking about it ever since. I wonder if that is how people see me, as a fat loser, only with the coffee coloured skin of a hybrid? Sometimes, when I am being honest, or just really mean with myself, that is how I see myself too. My mother hated the movie; I think on principle since I really loved it. Oh well, there is just no pleasing some people! I don't want to be a fat loser, desperate for any scrap of attention thrown my way. I don't want to be an embarrassment to Ronnie anymore because I am obese. I don't want to die young, or at all in fact, but most important of all, I do not want to give my mother the satisfaction of knowing how unhappy I am by constantly eating my feelings and staying fat and miserable.

Alice

Saturday 11 January

Dear Diary,

Although still pretty wheezy, I got up this morning and made myself put on my sneakers. I walked to the end of the corner of the street, about 800 metres, and then back home. It nearly killed me, and it took about half an hour, but I did it. I actually did it! Ronnie was so excited when I told him, he wants to come with me tomorrow, which I think is so sweet. Now if I can just learn to stomach broccoli! My mother was not impressed. She did her little nasal sniff, which I am sure she inherited from her own mother, when Ronnie and I were talking about my walk at the kitchen table. I sweetly suggested that she join us, as she too could certainly use the exercise. I was treated to a curse word and a badly aimed spoon thrown at my head! Unfortunately, later today I undid all of my good work walking by drinking a chocolate milkshake. Oh well, at least it is a start.

Alice

Sunday 12 January

Dear Diary,

Feeling pretty chuffed with myself right now. I got up this morning and again went straight out for a walk. I took Ronnie with me this time, it was nice just to talk with him without needing to watch what we said. We only went to the end of the street again, the same as yesterday, but it is better than nothing, which is what I have been doing for the rest of my life. I feel really self-conscious about walking, but at least it is better than joining a gym and having people mock me for my size. Actually, that is the main reason I have never exercised. The one and only time I went to a gym was for a yoga class, something that I used to love doing at home. I was feeling centred and happy, when I looked up in time to catch two skinny white bitches looking at me, talking and laughing, before turning away not at all concerned that they had been sprung. I never returned. Now here I am, almost two decades later, at five in the morning, wearing leggings and a long-sleeved tunic as it is the only piece of clothing I own that falls low enough past my stomach and butt for me to be comfortable walking in. On some level, I know that I shouldn't care what others think of me, but I do. I have spent my entire life trying to blend in, trying to be invisible in order to avoid the inevitable bullying, the harassment, the shame of being who I am. It is a hard habit to break.

Alice

Monday 13 January

Dear Diary,

I can't believe that the school holidays are nearly over, it seems like yesterday that they were beginning! I am really struggling to know what to do with Ronnie, he is so bright, but he is being stifled in his current school. I don't know if they don't want to help him advance, or if they just can't be bothered. I think it is the latter. They know he is autistic; they know he has a super high IQ, yet they give him a single worksheet to do in class and tell him to just draw when he is finished. What takes his peers all lesson to complete takes Ronnie ten minutes, maximum. My requests for extension work have fallen on deaf ears. His teacher actually admitted to me that she doesn't know what to do with him, that she has no work for his skill level. I stupidly thought that she would actually go and work out some lessons for him, but no, her solution is to let him do his own thing. Umm...I don't think so! She has had it in for him ever since he stood up in science class and told her that she was wrong. He was right, he usually always is, but she did not appreciate being corrected in front of the entire class. It scares me, the lack of quality teachers that are in the Alice Springs schools. They have set the bar so very low that it is no wonder that kids finish high school without even being able to read or write, or in a lot of cases, hold an intelligent conversation with someone. There is no way I will allow my son to be dragged down to the level the local school teaches at, no way at all! Options for a good education in Alice Springs are severely limited, I can homeschool via distance education with a school interstate – Queensland maybe – they have an exceptional education system, or I can send Ronnie away to boarding school, which is what most parents do. I really don't want to send my baby away, but I also don't want to hold him back. A lot to think about and a lot to look into. This is one of those days where I wish that I had a husband to talk things over with, I think it would be comforting.

Alice

Tuesday 14 January

Dear Diary,

As much as I loathe my co-workers, I really enjoy the actual job part, I just wish there were not so many politics involved. I also really enjoy the shift work side of things, I like working nights or evenings, it mixes up the monotony. The evenings are also fairly quiet, which gives me a chance to look up things online. I found a school in Queensland that sounds amazing, it is a gifted school, so naturally expensive, but it sounds like it would be worth it. I filled in the enrolment forms online and emailed them through tonight at work. I also spoke to Jenny, she was telling me that there is a school here in town that I should check out, they offer alternative education to kids who are unable to attend mainstream school for whatever reason. Apparently, there are gifted kids, delayed kids, teen mums, and kids on remand who all go there. Not completely sure that I want my son exposed to all of that mind you, but it is something to think about.

Alice

Wednesday 15 January

Dear Diary,

I can't believe that I have been for a walk every day for five days. Every. Single. Day. I feel so empowered and so darn proud of myself! I am yet to see any changes, but I am hanging in there. Various websites claim that once you start you are overwhelmed with energy and feel-good vibes. What crap, I have never been more tired in my life! I wonder how they get away with fake claims like that? Maybe if they have a chef, gardener, housekeeper, nanny, and so on, and maybe if they don't have to work, then yes, maybe they are full of energy, but not me. I am really struggling to stop eating rubbish. I want to give up coffee, sugar, bread, and pasta, but I haven't been able to bring myself to even try yet. One thing at a time. It is not helping that my mother is constantly buying junk food and bringing it into the house under the guise of buying me a treat. Firstly, she never buys me anything. Actually, she never buys anything at all, she merely adds it into my trolley and then walks away. And secondly, I have told her repeatedly that I am watching what I put into my body, but she just refuses to listen.

Alice

Thursday 16 January

Dear Diary,

Finally, some good news for Ronnie's schooling. The school I applied to in Queensland are happy to accept his enrolment, I just need to pay the tuition fee and we are all set. I also need to decide if I can bear to send him away to boarding school or if I should move with him. To move would mean quitting my job and selling my house, something that would not be easy in this town, especially with this house. I was such a sucker when I bought this house, I was just so desperate to have a home for Ronnie, to be safe, to not have to worry about constant homelessness, that I overlooked some of the issues with this place, and now I am stuck with it. Essentially, I purchased a house that is not to code and cannot be legally sold as-is. Joy. Moving away from here would mean walking away from my house and starting fresh elsewhere, assuming that I can cobble together enough of a deposit. Or it would mean moving and still maintaining the mortgage here, while I paid rent elsewhere. Obviously, with the issues in the house, it would not be rentable either, so no income coming in from it at all. I would do anything for Ronnie, without question, it is just going to be very hard emotionally and financially.

Alice

Friday 17 January

Dear Diary,

Last night at work was quiet enough for me to spend some time online researching my rights as far as

Ronnie's education. The Attorney General's website claims that every child in Australia is entitled to an education provided for them by the government and that the education shall be directed to the development of the child's personality, talents, and mental and physical abilities to their fullest potential. I decided to lodge an application for Ronnie at one of the local private schools, they have a scholarship program, so fingers crossed if he is accepted, he will qualify for one of them, as that will certainly help with the finances. If he doesn't qualify, I will just have to work extra hours to cover it. Nothing will stop me from giving Ronnie the education he deserves, not finances nor access. No way he gets passed over for a job or ends up in a dead-end admin position because he has no educational background. No way he struggles from payday to payday, no way he gives up on his dreams, no way in hell I sit back and allow him to end up like me. No way! That is the last thing I want for Ronnie, to have a lonely, sad, half-life where he is too scared to try. Or worse still, where the expectation of failure is so ingrained into him that he doesn't even know that he *can* try, that he *can* hope and aim for more, that he *does* deserve everything that he dreams of. The very thought of it keeps me awake at night, trying desperately to come up with a solution to try and protect him, to shield him from society's inevitable racist conclusions about him and his abilities, personality and employability.

Alice

Saturday 18 January

Dear Diary,

I spent most of the morning on social media, trawling through the buy, swap, sell ads, even though I don't actually need anything. I just find it so interesting, the things that people get rid of, and the reasons behind it. Despite not needing anything, I did find myself buying a couple of things, including a box of books for Ronnie and a super dooper gym standard treadmill for me. I nearly didn't buy the treadmill, the seller can't deliver, and I really did not want to have to ask Eric to collect it for me, lord knows that man doesn't need any encouragement! In the end, it was too good a price to pass up, especially with reports of dog attacks in the area, and I swallowed my misgivings and asked Eric if he would go and collect it for me. He agreed, as if he would ever refuse, and I took Ronnie with us as a chaperone. Every single thing about Eric makes my skin crawl, and despite my numerous attempts at educating him otherwise, he still seems to feel that it is completely appropriate to send me disgustingly lewd messages via text and social media. It is revolting! I always have to make sure that someone else is around whenever I see him, otherwise, he tries to put his filthy hands all over me. Even when there are people around, he still tries to pinch my butt. I mean, seriously, what woman appreciates having any part of her body pinched, especially against her will. Grow up! Anyhow, the treadmill is back here now, and I managed to successfully avoid having to ask Eric to stay for coffee, so win-win.

Alice

Sunday 19 January

Dear Diary,

Ronnie and I spent the day together, vegged out on the lounge. We watched some television, did some reading, and even played a couple of board games that we enjoy. I made us all some yummy steamed vegetables with a cheese sauce for dinner (naturally my mother complained about this as there was no meat, although she would also have complained if there was meat, as you can bet your bottom dollar that it would have been the wrong kind of meat, or not something that she wanted), and Ronnie and I snuggled and chatted before he went to bed. A perfectly perfect day.

Alice

Monday 20 January

Dear Diary,

I heard back from the local school today, they won't enrol Ronnie as he is too young. I am not sure when intelligence became directly related to age, but there you go. I think it is wrong of them to refuse his enrolment, and I think they are discriminating against him for being indigenous, and therefore, obviously, according to society, unable to be smart. I am going to appeal the decision with the education ombudsman, I think the decision is wrong. I feel a bit out of sorts tonight, no real reason, just blah. I have a dull ache in my left ovary, maybe my period is due? An early night for me I think, maybe a masturbation session, I haven't had one in a while, I just seem to be too tired to be bothered lately. I guess this must be what married couples feel like after a while? Still, it would be nice one day to find out, to actually have the chance to be married. Then again, in order for that to happen, I would first have to meet someone who wanted to marry me, and after thirty-five years I haven't even met anyone who wants to flirt with me, let alone ask me out on a date. Maybe if I were braver, or skinnier, or whiter, or any number of other things that I am not and never will be.

Alice

Tuesday 21 January

Dear Diary,

I had a call from the ombudsman's office, they agree that the decision to refuse enrolment was wrong and they referred me to the gifted children's program. I spoke to a lady called Carol, she was just lovely, and she has offered to lodge a formal investigation into the matter, which is nice. She was also telling me about the same local school that Jenny mentioned, was telling me that they are keen allies in helping gifted kids receive an education. She offered to send a letter of introduction via email if I was interested, which I said I was. It may make no difference, but it is worth a try.

Alice

Wednesday 22 January

Dear Diary,

Carol wasn't wrong about the local school being keen to help out. They called me first thing this morning to set up an appointment for tomorrow, apparently, Carol has forwarded them all of Ronnie's school reports, so the only thing we need to take with us is his birth certificate, should we decide to enrol him. Today was my dreaded long twelve-hour shift at work today, filling in for someone who is off sick. The plus side is that tomorrow is the start of my four days off, you have to love that! I love, love, love when my four days rostered off fall during the week, it means I can get so much more done! Tomorrow, after our school tour, I am hoping to look at universities online. I have been thinking of trying to enrol and maybe doing a course in social work, something that has high career prospects, but that also sounds interesting. Anything to better my work prospects really.

Alice

Thursday 23 January

Dear Diary,

Ronnie and I went down just after lunch today for the school tour. First impressions were not good, it looks like an absolute dump! In fact, I have been past there several times before and never even knew it was a school, I actually thought that it was an abandoned government building! Inside, however, is another story. It is huge and spacious, there are desks for each child, along with laptops and headsets. There is a kitchen and all food is provided. The kids do regular subjects like maths and English, but they also do leatherwork, chemistry and art. The kids are welcome to join in with the communal projects like building a pizza oven and raised garden beds, refurbishing a go-cart, and concreting. There are excursions each Monday for a barbecue lunch, and the food technology students prepare a three-course meal with cake whenever it is someone's birthday. The staff were all lovely and welcoming, and the kids all seemed perfectly normal and down to earth, regardless of what their past problems may have been. Ronnie and I both felt really happy being in that place, they were very respectful of our culture and heritage, as well as of Ronnie's needs. We decided to put in an application for Ronnie to start there next term, and the principal promised to let me know the outcome tomorrow.

Alice

Friday 24 January

Dear Diary,

True to her word, the principal called me today, Ronnie is enrolled in school for next term – finally! It is such a relief to me to have this all sorted out, I know he will be happy at this school, and best of all, we don't have to move! Not that I don't want to move, I would actually love to get out of this town, but the very thought terrifies me. Where could we go that would be safe? Western Australia is way too far away from civilisation for my liking, Victoria has too high a crime and drug presence for my peace of mind, South Australia is plagued with nasty bushfires each year, Queensland is prone to floods and damaging cyclones, the Australian Capital Territory is way too close-minded for me, Tasmania is not very good at being inclusive, and New South Wales...Actually, rural New

South Wales is somewhere where I could live quite happily, near Tamworth maybe, not too rural. As much as I yearn to move closer to a city, where there are museums and culture and opportunities for Ronnie, the reality is that I will most likely never move. For all the downfalls to living in Alice Springs, there is one major advantage, and that is that it is a very safe place to live. I have never once, in all my years of living here, felt in any way threatened. That peace, that safety, is something that I crave in my life.

Alice

Saturday 25 January

Dear Diary,

My fridge blew up today, in a cloud of smoke, that, had it not signalled a huge looming expense, would have been rather pretty to watch! Popped down to the local electronics store to choose a new one, oh my, there are so many pretty choices! I ummed and ahhed over them all – single doors, double doors, French doors, stainless steel, white, coloured, fridge/freezer combos, regular fridges, fridges without freezers at all. In the end, finances and common sense meant that I opted for a large fridge with a small freezer on top. I have a chest freezer for all of our bulk buys, so only really need a small top freezer for the meat that I plan to use each week, and maybe some ice cream for Ronnie in summer. They delivered it and were happy to take the old one away which was wonderful, as it meant I didn't need to ask Eric for his help. The new fridge works like a charm and is so quiet, I had to keep checking that it was actually running!

Alice

Sunday 26 January

Dear Diary,

After putting it off for a few days, I finally went online today and looked at university courses. I was hoping to apply on merit, but spaces are really limited. It looks like I will have to apply as a mature aged student, or as a bi-racial student, after all, something I did not want to have to do. It isn't that I am embarrassed to be Indigenous, or half Indigenous, I'm not, not really, it is just that I am so tired of everyone judging me on it and finding me lacking, or finding me worthy or extra concessions, as if being Indigenous is a disability. It isn't. Also, maybe I *am* a little bit ashamed. Ashamed of always being treated as a lesser class, as a second-rate citizen, or worse of all, being treated as a generalisation or a statistic. It doesn't help that my biological father refuses to acknowledge his Indigenous heritage, that his own biological mother drilled into him that it was something to be ashamed of, even though her relationship with his biological father had been a consensual, albeit adulterous, one. When my father left us for his mistress, my English born mother raised my siblings and I in a very English manner, and self-exploration or expression in any form was not something she encouraged with me at all. I would never have stood up to my mother as a child, I can't even stand up to her now as an adult, you can imagine how terrified I was of her as a child! I wish I knew why she hated me so much, why she continues to hate me so. It can't be a child thing, as she has two other children whom she always doted on. I used to think that perhaps I was adopted and that was why she didn't, or couldn't, love me as much as my siblings. Sadly, there is too much of a resemblance to her side of the family for me to ever have been adopted. I wish I knew who I was, I wish I didn't grapple with it so much. Maybe if I had a sense of self, I would find my sense of purpose, my place in this world. Perhaps then happiness would follow?

Alice

Monday 27 January

Dear Diary,

Ronnie started school today, he was so excited! He has skipped three grades and is starting out in grade seven, to begin with. There is no school uniform, so no mad rush to get the ironing sorted out. To be honest, I sort of missed that, the being needed. By all accounts, he loved his first day! No actual work was done, he will choose subjects tomorrow, but he went on an excursion and had a BBQ lunch, then just hung out and got to know everyone. I am really starting to feel the effects of my daily walk, I popped down to the shops today and while I was out, I ran into someone who I hadn't seen in months. She told me I looked really good, and, wait for it, actually asked for my advice about how she could get fit herself!! No one has ever asked me for fitness advice before, I was floored! I felt so chuffed I was inspired to go and buy a set of scales, which I did, so that I can track my weight as well as my distance and fitness. This is one gadget that I am determined to use, and not just have sit there collecting dust.

Alice

Tuesday 28 January

Dear Diary,

Ronnie got all set up today, he chose his subjects. He is doing Advanced Math, Advanced English, Digital Technologies, Visual Art, and Physics this semester. Hopefully, the workload won't be too much for him, he is only ten after all, despite how grown up he acts! Literally, every single thing is provided at this school. Textbooks? Check. Pens? Check. USB? Check. Slow-motion camera for recording physics data? Check. It really is amazing! All of Ronnie's classes are going to be online, through video link-up, so they set that up on his own – school-provided – laptop. Gosh, I wish this type of school had existed when I had been a child, I would have had a far happier school experience!

Alice

Wednesday 29 January

Dear Diary,

Such excitement in the house tonight! Ronnie mentioned to his school principal that he would love to learn to play an instrument, and he was offered a place in the music program. He was able to do his first pick, which was the guitar. He has his first lesson on Friday this week, apparently, the music teacher is based at one of the local public high schools and will travel to all of the government schools to provide students with private lessons. There is also a couple of bands that run during school time, that Ronnie can have the opportunity of joining if he wants to. They do performances at the end of the year for parents, and they also have the chance to take part in local eisteddfods. I am so glad that Ronnie wants to take music, it could be a real way for him to make friends and have a connection to people.

Alice

Thursday 30 January

Dear Diary,

As a surprise for Ronnie, after I dropped him off at school today, my mother and I went to the music shop where I purchased a new guitar for him. Nothing fancy, just a standard-sized guitar, but it is his own. I gave it to him when he got home from school, oh my god, he was so excited! He loves it, and spent ages dusting off imaginary dust and practising strumming the strings. Too stinking cute!

Alice

Friday 31 January

Dear Diary,

Ronnie had music as his last lesson of the day today, the only lesson where he has an actual teacher face to face, instead of via video link-up. When I picked him up, he was still in his lesson, it hadn't quite finished, and I was able to meet his music teacher in person. Oh. My. God! His music teacher is drop-dead sexy! It is actually Caleb, the student-teacher Ronnie had in his classroom a few years ago. If I had to design my dream guy, Caleb would be it. He has this really laid back, chilled vibe, and although I am not usually into it, he has shoulder-length hair that my fingers itch to run through. More importantly than anything else though, he has this presence, this essence of pure light that shines out of his face and surrounds everybody he comes into contact with. He has such a joy about him, he takes pleasure in listening to people, hearing their stories. His laugh is infectious, he has something nice to say about everybody, he makes people feel good just because he has the power to do so, without expecting anything back in return. He helps those less fortunate than himself to experience, and to tell their stories, through music. I have had a crush on him for years, ever since our orbits first crossed. I don't dare say anything, it is highly unlikely that he would ever feel the same way, presuming that he is not actually gay, married, or otherwise taken. It is nice though, knowing that I shall have the possibility of a glimpse of him to look forward to each Friday afternoon!

Alice

FEBRUARY

Saturday 1 February

Dear Diary,

Urgh, I hate February! My birthday month, the month of love and romance and other people living their happily ever after. It is not that I hate my birthday, or love, I don't. at least, not in theory. It is just that both of these things are so very hard for me to have to endure year after year, and I usually just end up spending the entire month feeling wretched. I really wish that things were different, I really wish that I didn't feel this way, but I do. I would like to think that I could still learn to love the month, that I could get to a point where it doesn't trigger me or make me extra sensitive and emotional, that somehow, I could learn to embrace it, but I think that I have left it too late. I try, I really do, for Ronnie's sake, not to get my hopes up too high, but the nearer my birthday draws, the more that small, secret, flame in my soul starts to grow, and the more that evil little voice inside my head, the soft, wistful one, starts to whisper to me...Maybe, maybe, maybe...What if? What if? What if? Maybe things will be different this year? Maybe people will remember your birthday, remember you? Maybe people will want to celebrate you, celebrate with you? What if you had a party? What if you made a fancy cake? What if you planned a nice dinner? Maybe, maybe, maybe...What if? What if? What if? Swirling round and round, like water escaping down a plug hole, never slowing, or stopping. The endless internal debate raging is exhausting, and I am left with little energy to do much more than my morning walk, a day at work, dinner with Ronnie and then, most nights, I am in bed by seven o'clock in the evening. Pathetic, lame, loser. This year I am going to try to fight it. I am going to try and retell the story in my head, try to silence the voices whispering to me. I think that the best thing to do is to simply not even acknowledge my birthday at all. It really does seem to be the epicentre of my distress each year, and the flashpoint for most of the conflict between my mother and I.

Alice

Sunday 2 February

Dear Diary,

Three people are away at work at the moment, three. That means that we are now down to two staff members, Sue and I, with both of us working constant twelve hours shifts, at least until the end of the week, when, hopefully, one of the other staff will be back from sick leave. It is so exhausting! I literally go to work, come home, sleep, then get up and go back to work. Sue and I get along really well, so we decided amongst ourselves who would do which shift. I took the night shift, as I prefer the solitude, and Sue would rather do days as there is no tedious filing to sort out. With only the two of us working, it means there are no breaks, so we either grab a few bites between phone calls or not at all. The joys of working a busy (and always understaffed) switchboard! As much as I do enjoy the variety of work that comes with my job, I must admit that I am growing tired of it. All I do is work. I never get to spend time with Ronnie. I wish I had more of a work-life balance. I wish I had a lot of things actually.

Alice

Monday 3 February

Dear Diary,

Night shift has given me way too much time on my hands to think. I am not sure that I will be in this position for much longer, at least, I really hope that I am not. I won't be able to get a fancy job for several years, it will take four years at university, and then I have to do a further two years of study or practical training, and then, if everything goes according to plan, I will be a psychologist. In the meantime, I would like a simple job, somewhere where I am actually valued as an employee, where my potential is recognised and nurtured. Is that too much to ask for? It clearly is in my current role; my boss is pissed with me because I told her I couldn't do any overtime this week. Honestly, isn't twelve hours a day enough? No way am I prepared to do sixteen, which is what she wanted. She was hoping that my shifts could overlap with Sue's so that we would be able to cover other staff members' lunch breaks! What a cheek! And she wonders why it is so hard for her to find, and retain, staff members. Honestly!

Alice

Tuesday 4 February

Dear Diary,

What a night! I feel like every second person who came to the switchboard to see me was coming to inform me of an upcoming holiday. Try as I might, it is hard not to feel a certain twinge of jealousy! I would give anything to be able to go on a holiday, to be able to take Ronnie away from Alice Springs, even if it is only for a short break, a week or two maybe. He dreams of going to Paris, of seeing the Eiffel Tower, ever since he was four and a pen pal sent me a postcard with the Eiffel Tower at night on the front, he has wanted to go. I would love to be able to take him, but, let's be honest, how many Indigenous people, or half Indigenous people, do you know who have travelled overseas? I don't imagine it would be many. Certainly not from Alice Springs in any case. Heck, you would be hard pushed to find us employed! Sarcastic much? It is what most people in town think, they are always so surprised when they encounter an aboriginal serving them in the supermarket or helping them in the dress shop. What do they think? What are they so afraid of? Do they expect a second head to sprout from our shoulders and devour their souls? While that would be pretty cool, sadly, it is not possible. I think I might try and put in for leave, maybe I will take Ronholidayolidays over Christmas. Surely by then, we won't be short-staffed anymore, and it will be okay for me to go away. If I get time tomorrow, I will check out flights and accommodation costs, maybe we can go someplace cold, someplace with snow. I've never had a white Christmas. Actually, I have never even seen snow, apart from on TV. A white Christmas would be really magical.

Alice

Wednesday 5 February

Dear Diary,

I found out that I got into university today, and I got my first preference! Ronnie was very excited when I told him at dinner, mother not so much. I guess it was no surprise really, that her first reaction was derision. Why bother studying now? Why psychology? Why not something practical, like business? How do I think I will be able to fit studying in? How am I going to pay for all of this? I had better not expect her to help me with Ronnie. Blah, blah, blah. Honestly, I am so proud of myself, especially as I never even finished high school. Not that I didn't want to mind you, I would have loved to, I certainly planned to graduate, unfortunately, I never had the chance. My mother needed someone to help her to pay her mortgage, and as the eldest, it fell to me. My biological sister, Amanda, the middle child, was the star of the family. She always had been, and it was clear to all that she was the favourite, she really could do no wrong. She had a manipulative streak that she inherited from our mother, a cleverness about her, she could make anyone do anything for her. It was a power she abused daily. Amanda was popular, she thrived on being noticed. She didn't care if you were a nice person if you had something that she could use, be it a fancy house with a pool or a brother she could be fuck buddies with, she was your best friend. As soon as she used up all of your resources, however, you were no longer of any interest to her. I expect that she would still be the same, I cut off all contact with her years ago, and have never looked back. Amanda was involved in everything. She did public speaking, swimming, netball, anything that put her centre stage. There was no way that it would have even occurred to my mother to ask Amanda to help out by getting an after-school job. No, the onus was on me, and the expectation was clear: leave school and get a job. I can still remember with perfect clarity, the day I knew that my dreams were pointless, worthless, nothing to even be considered or thought about by my mother. I was fifteen, unsure of myself in the world, battling a childhood that had been full of abuse and suffering. Desperate to please my mother, longing for her to show even the smallest scrap of love or affection towards me, I would never have even considered questioning her orders. So, with the signing of a form, she withdrew me from school. By the end of the following week, I had been employed by my local supermarket as a checkout operator. Me, the shyest person on earth. Ironic much! In theory, I should have been happy, after all, I had what most teenagers dream of, a job that paid well. Even as a junior, working full time meant that I took home around six hundred dollars each fortnight. At least, I should have taken that much home. Instead, my mother charged me three hundred dollars in rent each fortnight, plus one hundred dollars for food. Even that wasn't enough for her though, and she constantly 'borrowed' money from me, conveniently forgetting that it had been a loan whenever I requested repayment. The following year, my sister actually took a part-time job, and despite not being made to pay rent, was constantly broke and on the quest for a loan. Like the sucker I am, I lent her far too much money that I will never see returned. As well as working full time, getting home just before school ended meant that I was responsible for looking after my younger siblings and getting dinner started before my mother got home from work. Evening or online university classes were not heard of in early 2002, and so my dreams fell to the side. Once my father had put my siblings through university and they were both settled in jobs, I did think that it might have been my turn to chase after a dream and attend university, and I stupidly approached him to see if he would finance it, as he had for my siblings. He literally laughed in my face and told me, in front of my siblings in a crowded restaurant, and so matter of fact, that if I was really that determined to start studying, then he could probably contribute five hundred dollars towards the cost of a certificate course, but that would be all, I was not to ask for anything further. I didn't say another word for the rest of the meal, nor did I eat anything, my appetite having deserted me along with my courage. I didn't bother bringing it up again. So yeah, this is my time. And I am damn proud of myself!

Alice

Thursday 6 February

Dear Diary,

The university emailed me today, to let me know that there are dozens of scholarships available that I might want to apply for. Might?! Heck yes! I had no idea that there were so many, I printed off all of the details for the ones I am interested in applying for, I have the next few days off work, so will try and type up the first draft. It would be utterly amazing if I were able to get a scholarship, or even two! The guidelines say that you are able to accept a maximum of two scholarships, which seems fair enough. Gosh, it would make such a difference. Some of the scholarships are a combination of financial aid and work experience, others are financial aid and laptops, and some are just straight out financial aid, any of which would be greatly appreciated. If I were able to get a scholarship, it might mean that I am able to accept less overtime at work, which would give me more time at home with Ronnie, which is something that I crave. This week has been crazy at work, but thankfully, two of the staff that were off sick have returned, so both Sue and I now have the full weekend off, yay! Sue is even worse off than me, financially, so she doesn't turn down any shift if she is offered it, but gosh I am just so tired. I wish I could earn the same amount doing a regular seven-hour a day job, some cushy nine to five role, with weekends off. Oh well, a girl can dream, right?

Alice

Friday 7 February

Dear Diary,

Tomorrow is my birthday; I'll be thirty-five years old. It is hard to believe that I am this old really, to be honest, I am surprised that I lived past twenty-nine! No plans to do anything, obviously, I have never been someone others have considered worthy of celebrating. I did momentarily think about having a party, but seriously, who would I invite? Actually, I did ask a couple of acquaintances from work over for afternoon tea tomorrow, so we will see how that goes. If I get time in the morning, I might make a cake or something, we'll see what Ronnie feels like. Meanwhile, it is seven o'clock in the evening and I am having an early night. Pathetic? Yep. Depressing? More like depressed. I decided not to take Ronnie birthday present shopping this year, I just honestly could not face it. Every year it just gets me so upset. When I was a child and my parents divorced, making my mother a single parent, my grandmother would take my siblings and I all shopping for every special occasion, to buy a gift for our mother. When I had Ronnie, I wrongly assumed that my mother would take him gift shopping for me, but she was appalled with the idea. She told me flat out that she would never take him shopping, that she didn't see why she should have to take him shopping, that he isn't her child. So, for the past ten years, for every mother's day, birthday, Easter, and Christmas, I have gone gift shopping alone and chosen myself a gift. I have paid for it. I have wrapped it. I have given it to Ronnie to give back to me. I have acted surprised when I opened it. I just can't do it anymore. I am so tired of having to do everything myself. We shall see what tomorrow brings. I am trying not to get my hopes up too high, but I did make it clear that I would not be going shopping for my own gift this year, and I gave Ronnie and my mother enough warning, and enough money, that they should have had enough time to sort something out.

Alice

Saturday 8 February

Dear Diary,

Today was my birthday, or hell day as I refer to it. Every year I tell myself not to get my hopes up and every year I ignore my own advice. Oh, I don't mean to, it is just that I get so hopeful. So, it should be no real surprise to me then that my birthday is ruined every year. Every. Single. Year. To be fair, I don't have much to compare my birthday to. I have never been invited to a birthday party, or a birthday celebration of any kind, so all I know of birthdays is what I witnessed my sibling's birthdays to be, and of course, those I see on social media platforms, or on the television. I have never actually celebrated a birthday. In thirty-five years, I have had two birthday cakes, one birthday party, if you could call it that, and a handful of gifts. I have never had a birthday present that I wanted, or hoped for, or that I even actually had a need for unless it was something that I purchased myself for Ronnie to give to me. As a child, my mother would tell me that my birthday, being in February, fell way too close to Christmas for it to be possible to celebrate. It was not until I was in my early twenties that I realised that excuse was merely a cop-out. I had to watch as my siblings, who are born on the fifth and seventh of April, had a birthday celebration every single year. They were lucky enough to get it all. The birthday cakes they wanted. The birthday parties they wanted, for they never had to share, even being born only a day apart. They even had loads of friends bringing lots of amazing birthday gifts. And year after year I always got the exact same thing. Excuses. I did actually get a birthday gift from my mother and siblings when I turned ten. A sheet of teddy bear stickers. That was also the year that my mother allowed me to have my one and only birthday party, kind of. I had wanted to ask two girls from school to come over on a Friday afternoon and have a birthday cake. Mother, however, had other ideas. My mother invited all of the girls in my entire class. She went out and bought a pad of invitations from the supermarket, not the Barbie ones that I had coveted, but rather the plainer balloon themed invitations. She wrote them out carefully and even included a line all in capitals for the girls and their mothers to read: DO NOT BRING A BIRTHDAY GIFT, IT IS NOT REQUIRED. I smiled what my mother referred to as my idiot smile and pretended that I didn't notice what she had written. When the big day dawned, all of the girls showed up. My mother served all of my sibling's favourite foods, telling me that she chose what they liked as she knew that I would eat anything, I was such a little pig. My ever-clueless father had sent me some black, lacy underwear for my gift that year, and my mother thought it would be funny to hang them on our front picket fence for the entire small country town to see. When I got upset, my mother got annoyed, and I was sent to my room as punishment, only allowed out to say goodbye to my classmates, none of whom ever spoke to me again, not that I blame them. They had been exposed to the limelight that was my younger sister, and there was no way that I could ever hope to even come close to eclipsing that. I didn't even have a cake, my mother deciding not to bother making one as my sister had chosen to have sweet biscuits on the table instead. When I was thirteen my mother gave me another birthday present. A purple and black school bag, despite purple being my least favourite colour. Or maybe because of that? Then, for my eighteenth birthday, another gift, this time given jointly by my mother and my two siblings. A pair of women's white socks with cartoon teddy bears printed on them. I knew from the look on my mother's face when she gave the gift to me, a smug little smile, that it was going to be spiteful. To this day, I am so very glad that I schooled my expression into my carefully neutral face, practised during the years I have had to endure my mother. I am so glad that my mother, and both of my siblings, had work and school to go to that day. It left me in the house by myself, no surprise that I spent the entire day in floods of tears. That evening I received my first ever birthday cake. My mother had offered to make me one, so I requested plain chocolate, with chocolate icing. Simple. Fuss-free. Nothing fancy. She instead made me a banana cake, which I don't eat. She also took it upon herself to invite my sister's friend, a woman I cannot stand, and her two small children to join us. As the candles were lit, one of the kids sneezed all over the cake, so it ended up in the bin, something everyone except me found incredibly funny. Sometimes I wonder if that was a sign? A portent of my life to come. My twenty-first birthday was not much better. My mother and my sister had gone out to the local club for the evening, and my sister, the penultimate gambler, had won a four-day three-night holiday for four people to the sunshine coast in Queensland. My mother and my sister decided to go the following weekend, and they invited a couple of family friends to join them. Then they remembered it would be my twenty-first birthday. Awkward! My mother and my sister begrudgingly agreed that I could come as well, but that I would have to pay for the difference, which I did, stupid me! I also had the pleasure of taking us all out to a restaurant of my sister's choice for my birthday, followed by a trip to an ice cream parlour. I don't eat ice cream, never have. I spent all weekend schlepping around after them, at their beck and call. I still don't understand it. My siblings always had lovely gifts from our mother. At thirteen my sister received an emerald ring of her choice, at eighteen, a car. My brother a nice watch for his thirteenth, and also a car for his eighteenth. Less milestone birthdays netted them handbags and gaming systems, spa days and annual passes to the cinema. I stopped celebrating my birthday then until I had Ronnie. I thought it would be perfect, that I would finally have someone to celebrate with me. It was not. My mother still refuses to do anything to help. Goodness knows, this year I tried for weeks to get Ronnie and my mother interested in my birthday, but no. My mother is far too self-centred, all she wanted to talk about was her own birthday and how we should celebrate it, in August! So here I am, sitting here, pretending that it doesn't matter. Pretending that I don't care that once again I was not celebrated, or even remembered. Pretending that I don't care that my father didn't contact me. He never could remember my birthday; he would always call me a day late. Pretending that it doesn't hurt that after asking my mother to make a cake with Ronnie, and having to bribe her to agree, and after telling her exactly what I wanted (a simple orange cake with lemon icing), and after buying all of the ingredients, and after getting my hopes up that maybe today might actually be different, that I get a fruit cake. I don't even eat fruit cake. I never have. Mum does however and she wanted a piece. Fine. Don't. Fucking. Bother. So, I spent most of this morning baking. I made a batch of my famous fluffy cloud scones, a batch of egg salad ribbon sandwiches, some non-alcoholic punch, and, at Ronnie's request, a rainbow swirl vanilla cake. All while my mother stuffed her face with fruit cake and bemoaned the fact that I was actually having people over and that she would have to – gasp – have a shower and get dressed! I tried to get ready for my afternoon tea with cheeriness and not be bothered or upset, but the fact is, I was beyond hurt. Upon waking up today there was no gift from Ronnie or my mother, but worse, much, much, worse, there was no card from Ronnie. He always writes in a card for me, even if I do buy it myself. I am so upset right now; I just don't even have the words to try and explain just how hurt I am. I have never been celebrated. Is that normal? I honestly don't know; I literally have nothing to compare it to. Except for social media, and who really knows what the truth is on those sites? My mother does not understand the magnitude of my hurt in this regard. Is it unfounded? Am I being too high maintenance? Too needy? Too precious? Am I overreacting? I can't help the way I feel, no matter how inconvenient it is for my mother. I am so upset, I am sitting here ugly crying, trying to be quiet so that no one hears me. It is my own fault, I know that, it is always my own fault. So, this is it. The final straw. I am not ever going to acknowledge my birthday again. Ever. It is just too painful and disappointing for me to be constantly reminded of how very little I am wanted or how very little people think I am worth celebrating. I. am. Done.

Alice

Sunday 9 February

Dear Diary,

I wish I was normal. It is my biggest fear, not being normal. What is wrong with me? Sometimes I think that my chemical makeup has been altered, that there is something truly, genetically, wrong with me. I have a couple of memories from when I am five and six years old, nothing dramatic, but memories nonetheless. Me, walking home from kindergarten with my uncle, and getting a papercut from a painting that I was carrying. A car crash happening right outside our house in the middle of the night. Of going to some kind of lookout with my father's mother on Easter Sunday and being allowed a single Easter egg once there. Of losing my fifty-cent coin and being utterly devastated. Of being sick all over my brown school sandals. Of my favourite teacher, Mrs Hall, an aboriginal woman whom I adored. Like I said, nothing major, but memories nonetheless. And then, when I was seven years old, THE TRAUMA happened, and I think it permanently altered my brain. Since that event, I have been on high alert, constantly. I can't relax. I physically can't sleep for longer than five hours each night, no matter how hard I try, it is impossible. THE TRAUMA plays constantly on a loop in my head, not always at the front, sometimes buried down deep, but always there, playing on and on and on. Every time I think I have dealt with it or managed to suppress it far enough down to ignore it, it pops back up. A word or a sound or a smell and I am seven years old again. I wonder if that can happen, if a brain can really be altered by trauma. I guess there is no real point in wondering about it now, it is not as if it can ever be fixed.

Alice

Monday 10 February

Dear Diary,

I was reminded today of why I am loathe to leave the house, why I scurry so quickly in and out of the supermarket, my head down, trying to avoid all forms of eye contact. Why I shop quickly and race back to the safety of my house as fast as I can. People are so...rude? Mean? I am not sure really what the word is to use.

Why do absolute strangers feel it is appropriate, acceptable even, to comment on me and my looks? As if they have the right? As if they are entitled to know? At the supermarket today a lady told me that "you look very pretty in that dress, it's unusual for someone like you to dress so professionally, you don't often see it, do you? You're bi-racial, aren't you?" I could see her eyes studying my face, looking for the tell-tale indicators. I saw the shoppers at the neighbouring checkouts tilt their heads in my direction, knowing they were waiting for an answer, bemusement on their faces. I saw my son not even bat an eyelid, unaware that this woman was being rude, being racist, putting me down, intentionally. What the feck kind of message is that sending our kids? What the feck kind of message is that sending us? That we are less because of the colour of our skin? That our skin colour determines if we can dress nicely or not? That our skin colour dictates how nice people should be to us? Or how important we are? Or if we deserve to be treated as a human being or not? The sad thing is, I wanted to open my mouth and lie, to tell her that I was Australian, to ignore the comment about being bi-racial. Sometimes I am so ashamed of who I am, of what that makes me in the eyes of society. I don't want that for my son.

Alice

Tuesday 11 February

Dear Diary,

I am becoming increasingly unsettled with life in general. I wish I knew my history, knew who I was, who I came from. My father has not spoken to me in years, he never had a relationship with me, even as a child. It was always my siblings he was close to. Honestly, I have no idea what I did as a child, I have no memories of being with either my father or my mother. I must have been somewhere, right? Surely, I wasn't always left on my own, to amuse myself, was I? I know next to nothing about my father's history, only his mother's name, and his sister's name, neither of whom I have seen or heard from since I was a small child, although I do happen to know for a fact that they are still alive and well. In fact, the last time I saw my father's mother and sister, we had all gone out to dinner, to a place of their choosing. It was loud, full of smoke and drunk, brash men, and I hated it! Nothing on the menu appealed, so I ordered nothing. I don't drink, so was unable to get drunk with them. At the end of the night, I called them a taxi and went home. A couple of weeks later I got a very hurtful letter from them, telling me that they thought I had been so rude and wondering why I had even bothered to go in the first place. It stung! I still have it, and sometimes when I am feeling really crappy, I pull it out and read it, and remember what kind of stock I come from. It helps to know that I turned out this way, in part, due to those kinds of influences.

Alice

Wednesday 12 February

Dear Diary,

Can you believe it is Valentine's Day this week?! I would love to have a Valentine, one day, hopefully, I really will. People think I am joking when I tell them that I have never had a Valentine, they think I must be lying. Ha! If only they knew! Not only have I never had a Valentine, but I have never had anything, at all. I'm a virgin. I've never had sex or even been flirted with. I have never been kissed or had my hand held, or even been spoken to by a man in any other capacity other than professional. For whatever reason, I am not what men are drawn to. Maybe it's my weight, my tattoos, the fact I am old fashioned or can swear like a sailor, who knows. One thing is for sure, I won't let it stop me.

I don't think even my mother knows this, but I used a sample from a sperm donor and an In Vitro Fertilisation clinic to fall pregnant with Ronnie. Luckily for me, it worked the first time I tried. Does having Ronnie cure my longing to know what romantic love is for myself? No, but it gives me a focus and brings me joy. I know that I am a whole person without a man, I am not a fraction, but I long to know what it is like to simply hold someone's hand. It's not easy feeling out of sync with the world around you. It isn't that I am not attracted to men, I am. They just are not attracted to me. In fact, I wonder if they can actually even see me. My mother and father were the first two people to not want me. My mother will often tell the story of how she actually tried to leave me at the hospital. Born five weeks early, doctors had warned my mother that I would be mentally damaged, and to leave me. She agreed with them and was all set to walk out. My father refused to allow it. Ironic, as when I was thirteen, he told me that he was my biological father only and that if I ever wanted to see him again, I would have to pay for the airfares myself, as he lived in another state from where we lived. My aunt and uncle were the next people not to want me, refusing to billet me for a semester-long school exchange. Then, of course, there are all of the boys who never even saw me, but who I was acutely aware of. I can still remember the very first boy I ever noticed, properly noticed. Christopher Andrews. He had red hair and freckles and was the drummer at school. He taught me how to play a song that to this day, whenever I hear, reminds me of him. He was dating Rochelle Summers, a shy, bookish person. One day while watching him out of the window at school during textiles, I sewed straight through my finger and had to go up to the hospital for treatment. Next was James Barrwed, a guitarist. Sensing a theme?! James was as pasty white as they come and as skinny as a beanpole. It turns out that he was heavily into drugs, his mother rode in a bikie gang, terrifying woman as it happened. Quite lucky really that he wasn't interested in me. Several years later I found myself gawking after Michael Rankin. The aftermath of this crush was especially painful for me. I met him through the church, and he seemed genuine and nice. He said he wanted to get to know me, not rush into anything. He knew all the right things to say. He told me one day that he would marry me, not a proposal, more a statement of fact that this would occur in the future. No questions, just assumptions. It was around this time that I discovered just how underhanded he really was. He started talking about his future, about how I would support him to reach his dream (he was a music teacher with ideas of starting his own business) and then when he was established in a few years, we could think about looking at my dreams. Umm, no. if I have a relationship with someone, I fully expect us to work towards our dreams simultaneously. I started doubting him. maybe he sensed this? I don't know, but I do know that what happened next scarred me for years. He had a nervous breakdown. He called me in the night to tell me that God told him not to marry me. Okay, fair enough. That's done, I thought. Not so. I had his sisters, he had five, calling me in the middle of the night, screaming at me. They would come over to my house, banging on the door and windows. They trolled me on social media, made fake purchases from my online store, put in fake claims and feedback, left nasty reviews and comments about me all over my blog and other social media accounts. I was forced to close everything down. I actually had to change my name and move interstate to escape it all. It was horrific! And these were white people! Crazy! Happy to say, my next few crushes were a lot tamer. There was Daniel Johns, a co-worker. To be honest, I actually thought that he was flirting with me. He would lean close when we talked, he would always sit near me, he would laugh at my crappy jokes. Then he met Kelly, an acquaintance of mine, and also a co-worker, and that was that. I used to babysit her kids so that they could go off and have sex without being overheard. Daniel was another white guy, although at least he wasn't into music. Actually, all of the men I have ever had crushes on have all been white. I have no idea if that is a coincidence or a subconscious decision. There was the South African Niall, so yummy to look at, with a voice that flowed like molten lava. Eric Watkins could also go on this list, sort of. He is the only person to have ever claimed to want me, but he doesn't really. What he wants is my body. He sends me endless messages on social media and my mobile, detailing exactly what he wants to do to me, not with me, to me, and where, and with what and for how long. It is so insidiously revolting! Just seeing his name pop up on the screen makes my skin crawl. No matter how many times I tell him to stop, he keeps persisting. Then, lastly, there is Caleb Granger. I have liked this man for years. In actual fact, there is a very large part of me that honestly believes that he is my soul mate, as crazy as that sounds. When I see him, I see how he is in years from now. I can literally see us growing old together. I know there is no way that would ever happen, he doesn't like me, I don't think he even sees me. But still...I think it and I dream it. I have stopped trying to meet someone. I just know that he is meant for me, and if I can't have him, I don't want anybody else. I don't want to settle. I want the fairy-tale, no matter how old fashioned or childish it is. I want someone whose breath catches when I walk into the room. I want someone who helps to build me up instead of tearing me down. Someone who defends and fights for me if I need them to. I want it all. I want to be loved and cherished and needed and wanted. I wish that was a realistic hope, I really do, it hurts, physically aches, to know that it is never going to be a reality for me.

Alice

Thursday 13 February

Dear Diary,

There are so many things I have never done. Not for a lack of interest, oh the interest is there, I have just never had the opportunity, my life being what it is. I have never had my hands held lovingly, or in comfort. I have never been kissed, other than platonically. So what you say, there is plenty of time. I am 35. No wolf whistles or cheeky winks, no cheesy pickup lines for me. Embarrassed to say, I have never spoken to a man that way. Or at all, except in the course of a working day. I have never been smiled at or even seen. A life lived under the cloak of invisibility. What is it that makes me a pariah, undesirable to men? Is it my old double-edged sword, my weight? I exercise daily yet I am still fat. Am I undesirable because I don't? I don't smoke or drink, and drugs aren't my thing. I am fading away; I just want to be seen. Am I too nice? Too shy? Was I born in the wrong era? Am I too old fashioned? Is it my teeth? How does it feel, I need to know. A yearning ache so strong I can taste it. I wish I knew. I just wish I could experience the sensation, of holding someone's hand. Of touch, of being embraced. Of being wanted, needed, desired. I would even pay someone, to sit next to me and hold my hand. Even in silence, how pathetic is that? How desperately lonely I am. Sometimes I think that I must literally be, the loneliest person in the world.

Alice

Friday 14 February

Dear Diary,

Today is Valentine's Day. I got up early today and made a batch of heart-shaped pikelets for Ronnie for breakfast. It was actually a lot harder to make them than I thought it would be! He is totally worth it though. The school went on an excursion today, down to a local waterhole. They had a BBQ with kangaroo tail and steak for lunch, with various salads and rolls. One of the food technology students even made a chocolate mud cake to take down for dessert, which, according to Ronnie, was super yummy! Ronnie had a really great time today, and he was even back in time for his music lesson, which meant that I got a sneaky little Valentine's Day gift of my own when I watched Caleb come out of class with Ronnie. Honestly, seeing Caleb makes my heart both warm and ache all at once. I wonder what it would feel like, to actually have a man like Caleb look at me, really look at me, and actually see me for who I am. Would he smile? Or would he laugh at me? Last year I was at a local chicken restaurant with Ronnie and there was a car going through the drive-thru. There was a man in the driver's seat looking into the restaurant, so I smiled at him. He looked me straight in the eye and laughed, shaking his head as he mouthed "not a chance". I was so embarrassed. My insides went stone cold, and I tried not to let it show, I pretended that I hadn't noticed, that I had been smiling at Ronnie and not at him. Ronnie noticed though; he always notices. He stopped talking and leant over the table to hold my hand. I wish I knew why I am so unwanted. Why doesn't anyone want me? I'm thirty-five years old for goodness sake, and the only person I know who is still a virgin. Talk about a loser! I've never had sex or even been flirted with. For whatever reason, I am not what men are drawn to. Maybe it's my weight, my tattoos, the fact I am old fashioned or can swear like a sailor, who knows. It is so easy to pretend that I am a whole person without a man in my life, that I am not a fraction of a person just because I am single, but the actual, physical pain that I feel on a daily basis from the simple act of being unwanted, is overwhelming. I have spent thirty-five years feeling out of sync with the rest of the world. So desperate for someone to love, and for someone to love me, that I used an In Vitro Fertilisation clinic and a sperm donor in order to have my precious Ronnie. And while I long to know what it is like to simply hold someone's hand, it is unlikely to happen, so instead, I pour all of my love and focus into Ronnie. Does it cure my longing to know what love is for myself? No, but it gives me a focus and brings me joy. After spending the afternoon trawling through social media and seeing all of the status updates about people's perfect gifts and plans and lives, I was too depressed to cook, so I made frozen pizza for dinner, I just couldn't be bothered putting any effort in tonight.

Once Ronnie is in bed I think I will turn in as well, I need to have a decent cry, and I refuse to cry in front of Ronnie.

Alice

Saturday 15 February

Dear Diary,

I went shopping today, just to get some general stuff. I bought Ronnie a pair of new shoes for school (oh my gosh, this boy goes through shoes quicker than most people go through milk!) and picked up a booklet of postage stamps. Then I stopped off at the supermarket to grab some groceries, nothing major, just a handful of items we had run out of. I spent so much money, I overspent the food budget by $70! I have no idea when food became so very expensive. I mean, seriously, $70 for literally milk, bread, meat and some fruit. Insane! I am really scared tonight; I just don't know what to do. I have next to no savings left; I am really worried. I don't know how I will manage to pay for everything. I have bills due soon, and my mother needs her medication for her arthritis. It is just one thing after another lately.

Alice

Sunday 16 February

Dear Diary,

I am really upset tonight, so very stressed out about money. I work myself to the bone, yet it is never enough. This house is falling apart around my ears. This morning the knob of the bathroom door shattered, and then the toaster stopped working. Great, just more things to add to my ever-growing list of items to be fixed or replaced around this crap house. I will probably still be living here when I am old and half dead, still trying to fix things and keep it running in a mostly liveable condition. I wish I had never bought this stupid house! I wish I had never moved to this rubbish town, I wish that I had never allowed mother to guilt me into moving here so that she could afford to stay here, so that I could help her with the rent in this town. I smiled at someone at work today, and they looked at me with a confused expression on their face, as if they were not sure why on earth I would be smiling at them. They drew their eyebrows together and shook their head as if dispelling the remnants of a foggy dream. I excused myself to go to the bathroom so that I could look in the mirror and try to see what it was that they had seen. I saw me. Fat. Baggy cheeks. Crooked teeth. Double chin. Okay, triple chin. Ugly. Old. A chill crept right into my soul during my scrutiny and stuck with me all day. No wonder I am alone. No wonder I am lonely. My mother was right, her daily taunts of me were spot on. Who on earth would ever want someone like me? Who on earth could ever love someone like me? I loathe myself. I loathe every single thing about me. I am so lonely.

Alice

Monday 17 February

Dear Diary,

Urgh! I am glad today is over. I was actually having a mostly okay day at work, when, during a super quiet moment, I made the fatal error of checking my social media account. There was a private message there from one of the admins of a group I am in, telling me that a post of mine had been removed, as it had been very rude, and the admins were now going to meet to discuss it. I literally copied and pasted the exact same thing as someone else had done; the only difference is that the other poster is a close friend with some of the admin, and I am not a suck-up. I am so over it, the double standards. I am so tired of trying to fit in. I only have myself to blame, I know that, I keep trying to make friends, instead of just accepting facts. I am a loser. People like me are not meant to have friends. My whole life I have been trying to make a friend. Just one. Singular. I am not greedy, I just want one, solitary friend. You would have thought that I would have learnt my lesson by now.

Alice

Tuesday 18 February

Dear Diary,

I took Ronnie to the dentist today for a check-up. He needs to go back next week for two fillings, one small, one not so small. He is not looking forward to that, as it will most likely mean a needle, but I told him that he is lucky. Lucky to have a mother who cares so much about his oral hygiene. When I was a child, I had dreadful teeth, and my mother refused to do anything to help me. One of my teeth got badly abscessed and needed to be removed, and she refused to do anything about it. My teacher actually sent me to the school dentist on one of their visiting days, and he then called my mother to come and take me home early it had been so bad. I was also put on the waiting list for braces, and when I reached the top of the list, my mother refused to take me. She merely ripped the letter up and threw it in the bin. I asked her once about my appointment and she told me there was no point in going, it wasn't as if anyone would ever want to see me smile. She was right about that, no one wants to see me smile, certainly not with horror story teeth like mine. It is too late to fix them now, even if I had the money, they are so badly deformed and rotted away. It is a huge embarrassment to me, I am so ashamed whenever I find myself smiling in public, it is mortifying to me, the possibility that someone might have seen my smile. It was par for the course really; my mother was not one for any kind of health care. For heaven's sake, she never even gave me the period or sex talk! I got my period when I was thirteen, I discovered it when I went to get into the shower before school. I didn't say anything. Why would I? My mother had never mentioned it, so I assumed that it was something to be ashamed of, something to ignore, to brush under the carpet. I will never forget the shame I felt at having to buy my own sanitary pads. Yes, I had to buy them. My mother informed me that she didn't use them so why should she buy them? She wouldn't even go into the supermarket with me. Even to this day, my face flames when I think about it. I was almost in tears my first time, thankfully a nice, older lady walking past asked if I needed help. It was so awkward. My mother had given me very little money, I had to get no-name sanitary pads, which I am sure are fine, but they really don't do anything for someone's self-confidence! Especially when my sister was allowed to buy top of the line sanitary napkins as she refused to use what she called poverty ones. And now, whenever I need to buy tampons, I just rush past them and throw a box in, barely looking at them, so convinced I am, that I am being judged and watched. As for sex, ha! You only have to watch how blushingly awkward I am around a man to know that I never had that talk. Maybe she thought there was no point, so convinced she was that no one would ever want me. Maybe she thought the male would take the lead? I don't know. In any case, idle curiosity about just what it was that I was missing led me to do an internet search a few years ago. What an eye-opener that was! Holey moley! I knew the basic mechanics of sex, but never did I imagine there to be so many different positions or varieties. It was mind-blowing. Rather moot really, as it seems quite unlikely that I shall ever have the chance to experience sex for myself, other than through masturbation. Maybe when Ronnie is grown up and flown the nest, maybe I will be brave and find a male prostitute with a penchant for old women. Actually, probably not. The whole idea sounds really seedy and kinda gross. No, I guess it is just not meant to be for me. Surely, I can't possibly be the only person alive who has never, ever had sex? Surely if I die a virgin, I won't be the first to do so? I wonder if my mother knew this about me if she would be happy? Genuinely happy? I imagine she would be. Looking back, the only thing my mother actually taught me in life was how to hate myself. In that lesson, she really excelled!

Alice

Thursday 20 February

Dear Diary,

Ronnie was back at the doctor today, one of his knees will often swell up for no reason, and he generally gets a bit of a temperature when it happens as well. The doctor had a good look and has decided to refer Ronnie for further tests, including blood tests to determine his white blood cell count, and to check for any inflammation markers, which might then signify that he has juvenile arthritis. It is a bit scary for me, as the only reason that I know of for kids to random swell at the joints is if they have leukemia. So, we went straight from the doctor to the pathology unit for the blood tests, and we will go back next week sometime for the results.

Alice

Saturday 22 February

Dear Diary,

I saw Caleb at the library today, and he completely ignored me which stung. I saw him look around the room, his eyes grazing straight over my face, with not a flicker of recognition or acknowledgment. He didn't see me, not really, to him I was invisible. Shoulders slumped, I left the library, obsessing and reliving the encounter, again and again, all day, growing colder and colder inside with each replay.

Alice

Thursday 27 February

Dear Diary,

Ever the dreamer, I splurged on a lotto ticket today, something I rarely do and really shouldn't have done. Logically I know it is a waste of money, that the odds are astronomically stacked against me winning, but the hopeful, wistful part of my brain argues that why shouldn't I win? Someone has to win, and if I don't buy a ticket, I have zero chance, at least with a ticket I have some chance.

Alice

Friday 28 February

Dear Diary,

When my eyes are blurry with tiredness and I catch sight of myself in the mirror, I stop surprised, struck with how pretty I am. My skin is soft, hair pixie, eyes sparkle. I wish I knew how to see that version of me when I was fully awake, how to make other people see that version of me.

Alice

MARCH

Sunday 1 March

Dear Diary,

Another disgusting text message from Eric, seriously, when will he get the message! If he isn't texting me, he is messaging me on social media. He is an absolute creep; he makes my skin crawl. My first job in Alice Springs was running the holiday program at the local shopping centre, and he was technically my superior. He had my phone number in case of a shift change or other work-related calamity, but now, years later, only uses it to harass me. Mostly I delete his texts and social media messages unread, but very, very occasionally I make the mistake of actually reading them, something that I always instantly regret.

Alice

Monday 2 March

Dear Diary,

My university course started today. I am doing the entire degree externally, as I still need to be able to work and pay my bills. I wasn't sure what to expect from my first class, even though it was recorded earlier and uploaded to the server, I was still nervous. It went well, the first couple of subjects all seem to be about discovering my learning style and creating a learning plan to help me reach my goals, basic stuff, which is a relief. I haven't studied in two decades, I was so worried I would be the dumb one in the class, it is nice to find that is not the case. The classes are three nights a week, all pre-recorded so that I can watch them when it is convenient to me, which I like. Ronnie is so excited for me, he wanted to hear all about my first lesson, the sweetheart. I am hoping that I do well this semester, it might make all the difference as to whether or not I keep going ahead with my studies.

Alice

Tuesday 3 March

Dear Diary,

I have always thought of March as rather a dull and dreary month, nothing much ever happens in March. At least, nothing much happens in my world in any case. I am trying very hard to keep a steady and accurate account of my year, I find it hard to remember to write in a diary at times, and usually, when I do remember, I am just too tired to be bothered, but not this year. This year I am determined, no matter how boring the month is!

Alice

Wednesday 4 March

Dear Diary,

Eric texted me again today. Sometimes I am really not sure what to do about him. I have told him not to text me, not to send me any messages or photos through social media, that they then show up on my mobile phone that anyone can access, but he just doesn't listen. I don't know if he doesn't listen because he doesn't want to, or if he forgets what I have told him, or if he just simply does not care about what I want. It is disgusting, the things he sends me. He acts as if he owns me, or as if we have some kind of understanding in place. I worked with him for three weeks, years ago, and now he acts as if we had some great romance or relationship or friendship, none of which we had, or ever will have. I am sure he is probably a nice person, I just feel uncomfortable around him, slimy and in need of a shower. It might not be that way if he and I had anything in common, but we don't. He is older than I am, maybe in his late fifties or early sixties. He seems to only ever think about sex, is that a guy thing? Or a creep thing? Either way, his messages leave nothing to the imagination, he seems to have a variety of sex toys and tools and lets me know in graphic detail just exactly what he would like to be doing to me, not with me, but to me. Twisted fantasies are fine if there are two consenting adult partners, but when it is one-sided it creeps me out.

Alice

Thursday 5 March

Dear Diary,

Ronnie and I went back to the doctor today, his blood test results are back, and thankfully, there is nothing seriously wrong. The doctor has referred us to the paediatrician at the hospital, for further tests, but he thinks the result will be that Ronnie has Chronic Fatigue Syndrome, which is not great, but a lot better than what it might have been.

Alice

Friday 6 March

Dear Diary,

I saw Caleb again today; gosh he looks good! Whoever has married him certainly got lucky. I wish that I had that, a marriage, someone to talk to. I'm not an idiot, I know not every marriage is sunshine and roses, sometimes I think that I would be okay with settling for less. I'm almost ashamed to admit it, but I would marry someone that I didn't love, that I wasn't attracted to, heck, I would marry someone who didn't love me either. As long as they would accept my son into their family, as long as they could provide companionship and friendship, and security, then I would be okay. I have been alone and lonely for too long, and all I see ahead of me is endless years of loneliness and fear, a lonely, empty life spent watching everybody else live. I don't want that.

Alice

Saturday 7 March

Dear Diary,

I had an email at work today saying that my leave has been granted, so that is nice. I have four weeks off over Christmas, as well as my usually rostered days off, so thirty-five days altogether. I'm not sure where we will go or what we will do, but I am determined to take Ronnie away on holiday.

Alice

Sunday 8 March

Dear Diary,

The wretched toaster died today, although to be fair, it did have help. My interfering mother decided that there was no way that I had actually cleaned the toaster like I said I had, so she washed it herself. In hot soapy water. When she plugged it back in and turned it on there was an ominous pfft, and then nothing. She tripped the safety switch in the fuse box, and once it was back on, the toaster was nonresponsive. Apparently, she cannot live without a toaster in the house, so we went down to the local department store to buy a new one. She was eyeing off a pastel blue brand name toaster, as if I could ever afford to buy that! I chose a simple white toaster for seven dollars, as far as I am concerned, a toaster is a toaster, they all do the same job.

Alice

Friday 13 March

Dear Diary,

I managed to totally embarrass myself today, without really even trying to. I didn't even realise that I was doing it until later. I went to collect Ronnie from school and being a Friday, his last lesson was music. He came out with Caleb, still talking away animatedly. I could not keep my eyes off Caleb, it was a potent mix, of skinny black jeans and boots combined with his scruffy trademark shoulder-length hair. It made my throat ache with all the unspoken words he would never hear; all the things I wish I was brave enough to tell him. once Ronnie got in the car, he told me that I looked nice and asked if we were going somewhere. I know how he hates to go out without prior warning, so I assured him that we were going straight home. He looked at me puzzled and asked me why I was dressed up then. I hadn't actually noticed that I was until he mentioned it, but he was right, I was dressed up. I had my nice dress on, the floral one that is usually only reserved for school meetings and grocery shopping, when I need to look important and educated. I cringed when I realised that not only had I dressed up but that I had also added some basic make-up, something that I never wear unless I need to make a massively good impression. It was just some translucent powder and clear mascara, but still...It wasn't until we were halfway home, Ronnie lost in thought, that he asked me quietly if I liked Caleb. I was mortified! If Ronnie had picked up on that, who else had? I told Ronnie that yes, I did like Caleb, that he was a decent human being, and that finding men like that was rare. I'm going to have to be super careful how I act towards Caleb now that Ronnie knows that I have a soft spot for him.

Alice

Saturday 14 March

Dear Diary,

Eric has been messaging me most of the day, a combination of smutty, disgusting text messages, and weird, banal, mundane text messages. At various points throughout the day, he was texting me that his dog is crazy, that the weather was hot, and that he was stroking himself while thinking of me (WTF?! Are there actually women out there that enjoy hearing this kind of filth?). it just makes for a really tiring and stressful day. After lunchtime I stopped reading his messages, I just deleted them without opening them.

Alice

Sunday 15 March

Dear Diary,

I'm glad I sleep with my mobile switched to silent, Eric sent me nearly a dozen text messages last night, all of which I deleted unread this morning before blocking his phone number from my mobile phone. I think I need to be harsher with him in terms of what I find acceptable or not, and if he still refuses to listen, I think I will find a way to block him from contacting me on social media.

Alice

Wednesday 18 March

Dear Diary,

My sodding electric frying pan stopped working today, right in the middle of me cooking dinner. Grrr! I just tipped it all into a saucepan and finished cooking it on the stovetop, but it is just annoying, why do appliances all seem to break at the same time? I tend to use my electric frying pan several times a week, it is too hot to have the oven or stove on, so I will need to get it replaced as soon as possible.

Alice

Friday 20 March

Dear Diary,

I made sure that I did not dress up to collect Ronnie from school today. After last week, I wasn't going to take any chances. I deliberately wore leggings paired with a tunic that I have had for a thousand years, and when Ronnie came out with Caleb, I made sure that I waved at Ronnie and then I turned away, pretending to talk on my mobile phone until he got in the car. I didn't want to give myself any chance to make eye contact, or to talk, or to otherwise embarrass myself in front of Caleb. If he knew that I had a crush on him, I would be mortified!

Alice

Saturday 21 March

Dear Diary,

We had to go into town this morning, well actually, we didn't need to, my mother could have picked up my two grocery items when she went to buy milk, but she is in another one of her epic moods, and refused, so we all had to pile into the car to go to town. On the way there we stopped at a red light, and a car turned the corner in front of us. It was Caleb, and there was a woman in the front passenger seat, at nine o'clock in the morning on a Saturday. He was obviously driving her home after spending the night with him, or maybe she is his wife or girlfriend. They were both laughing, not in a flirty way, but in a throw your head back raucous kind of way, it made it look as if they were very familiar with each other. She was so pretty, skinny, obviously, you don't even get the slightest look unless you are less than a size twelve these days, with brown hair and a sweet pixie face. She is probably such a nice person, not that I will ever know, I only saw her for a few moments as they passed, but it was enough to make me feel like crap. My face flamed, I had to turn my head away before my mother commented on my appearance yet again, and my insides turned ice-cold, almost as if I was filled with dread. I tried to shake it off, I really did, but it played on my mind all day. My insides are still cold.

Alice

Sunday 22 March

Dear Diary,

Do you think it is too much to hope for happiness? Real happiness that sprouts from your soul and shines like moonbeams out of your face? I am starting to think that happiness is just an illusion, carefully cultivated by people so as not to show their real lives. I don't think that I have ever actually been happy. When I think over the events in my life that might have been happy, there is always a shadow being cast over them, tainting them. Am I not capable of being happy? Sometimes I wonder. My life has been so hard, so painful, full of hardships and neglect, that I wonder if I would even recognise happiness if it was a gift wrapped and handed to me. I think that happiness means something different to everyone, but for me, happiness would mean not having to struggle, it would mean friendship and love, acceptance and support, a lightness to my life. I think I have left it too late, and that fills me with such intense feelings of grief.

Alice

Tuesday 24 March

Dear Diary,

Ronnie and I saw the paediatrician at the hospital today, and she was in agreeance with the doctor, Ronnie has Chronic Fatigue Syndrome. Ironically enough, she believes that it was triggered by his recent general anaesthetic for a foot operation, which might explain why he then suffered six weeks of infections. There is no cure as such, some people overcome it, others learn to live with it. Exercise won't help, despite what my mother seems to think, neither will lots of leafy green vegetables.

Alice

Thursday 26 March

Dear Diary,

I woke to a barrage of messages from Eric today. Again. I just can't face them, honestly, I just can't. I spent the morning typing up a reply to him, telling him again that I don't like these messages, that he needs to stop sending them to, that what he wants to do to me is not something that I would ever willingly be a part of. I was as blunt as I could be without being too rude. I used simple, clear language so that there would be no misunderstandings on his part, and then I sent it. In return, I received a message that was essentially a pornographic short story. So, he obviously is not interested in what I want. I just want to crawl into bed and cry. Why is it that the only man who has ever wanted me, only wants to do disgusting acts to me, is only interested in humiliating and degrading me?

Alice

Friday 27 March

Dear Diary,

Today at work one of the ladies in my office received a bunch of flowers, it wasn't even her birthday. No one had died, she hadn't been promoted or fired, she simply received them because someone in the world feels that she is deserving of love and affection. I tried to be happy for her, but as I exclaimed over her flowers my voice sounded wistful even to my ears. I found I needed to go to the bathroom and swallow thickly so as not to cry, how stupid is that? It always happens like this, my yearning and wistfulness for things I have never had nor am likely to get, always strikes when I least expect it. They were beautiful flowers. I wish I could be sent flowers. I have never had any flowers given to me, not even when my son was born, although I guess that doesn't really count as no one came to visit me in the hospital while I was there. Still, even when we returned home there were no flower deliveries, no cards of congratulations, nothing. No flowers on any of my birthdays, nor Valentine's Day, nothing. It really helps to ram home the message that I am just not worth it.

Alice

Tuesday 31 March

Dear Diary,

I am so glad that this month is over, I wish the whole year were over, to be honest. I feel that so far this year I am yet to achieve anything that I set out to try and do. I feel like such a failure. What the hell is wrong with me? Well, apart from the obvious of course. I saw myself in the mirror today, I was so disgusted with myself. Fat. Ugly. I sometimes think that my mother was right. Who would ever want someone like me?!

Alice

APRIL

Wednesday 1 April

Dear Diary,

April fool's day today, which meant that work was an absolute nightmare! As usual, the office clique decided it would be hilarious to play a prank on me, and despite me being on high alert today, I didn't even see it coming. I received an official typed letter on letterhead from my actual boss, letting me know that I was to complete all the filing and keep a log of all the calls I took and tasks that I did today, as she had received a number of complaints from other personnel within the building, saying that I spent most of my shifts talking and barely got any work done. I was mortified when I read it, I knew my face was going to be flaming red.so I logged everything that I did, and at the end of the day I went to her office to give her my log and she had no idea what I was talking about. She was confused as to why I would be showing her the log, reminding me that everyone knew their roles and that trying to implement something like this was unnecessary, and to be frank, rather over my head. I was so embarrassed. I stood there listening to her lecture, wishing the floor would open up and swallow me whole. When I returned to the office, the ladies were all gathered in a group, whispering furiously, scattering when they saw me, barely hiding their smirks. I didn't say another word, I simply switched off the computer, gathered my bag together, and headed out the door. As the door closed, I heard them all burst into gales of laughter. I loathe my job and the cows that work there with me.

Alice

Thursday 2 April

Dear Diary,

I thought it would be nice for Easter to have a few people over for brunch, and maybe have an Easter egg hunt. So anyway, I invited a few people that I know, mostly old work colleagues and some of my mother's friends, and I tried not to get too excited, and then by the end of the day, every single person I had asked had already replied to say that they were unable to come. Apparently, they all had other plans, at least that's what they said. That's what they always say. Honestly, I don't even know why I bother asking people to do anything with me anymore, all it ever does is make me upset.

Alice

Friday 3 April

Dear Diary,

I got into trouble today, well not trouble exactly, more chastised, and then humiliated. I am in a group on social media, for women only, where they can trade and swap and do tags. Anyway, I joined the group in the hopes that I would make a friend, but it didn't work out like that. Everyone is so cliquey, and I just don't seem to be able to fit in anywhere. Take the tags, for example, they are pretty straightforward. You tag the person above you and send them whatever the tag is for. Someone then tags you and so on. All of the tags have a minimum spend of two dollars, and a maximum spend of five dollars. Supposedly. I thought that was good because I'm on a fixed income, but unfortunately, no one else in the group seems to spend that amount of money, they all spend way more than the maximum. So, then it looks like I have spent not enough money, as if I haven't put any effort in or thought into what I have sent. It is just really embarrassing. Some of the tags are for things like sending somebody a surprise from their wish list. Now, the wish list is meant to contain items under five dollars, but they don't of course. The group has admin officers and they always manage to tag each other and to send to each other for all of the swaps. Rigged, much?! They are the worst offenders; they always send hideously expensive items to each other. I'm talking about items like a brand name coffee maker, or a leather handbag, or a pair of pearl earrings, or boxes full of craft supplies. So, I sent an Australian mad Canadian admin officer a packet of Australian themed temporary tattoos, and then today I see in the group that I have been tagged in a group post. Lo and behold, it is chastising me, as she considers temporary tattoos to be stickers, which are on her do not send list. Now I am required to resend her an item that is appropriate. Although I was embarrassed to have been publicly called out, and I could feel the coldness seeping through my chest, I did try to brush it off and thought that I would go ahead and participate in the weekly wishes, at least by sending some, I don't often post a request for wishes as I am not usually chosen. I commented that I would grant a wish for Julie. Another eight people also said that they would grant her a wish. She then went ahead and replied after every single message with a thank you and a heart emoji. Except on mine. On mine, all she did was give it a like. Talk about an obvious and open snub. It actually really hurt my feelings, which I know sounds stupid.

Alice

Saturday 4 April

Dear Diary,

Talk about surprised, I got an Easter present from Eric today. Honestly, will he ever get the message?! Every single thing about him grosses me out. I don't know why he bothers, all it does is make me annoyed, and it's not as if it is anything that I want anyway, how could it be when he doesn't know me or anything about me? Honestly, I know that I should probably be grateful that somebody has remembered me but seriously nothing he ever does comes without strings attached. It really exhausts me constantly fending him off.

Alice

Sunday 5 April

Dear Diary,

Easter Sunday today. Nothing exciting happening in my world, I organised an Easter egg hunt for Ronnie, our annual tradition. Instead of just hiding the eggs, I hide the eggs and then give him a cryptic clue, which then leads to an egg and another cryptic clue and so on. He loves it, and every year he begs me to make it harder and harder for him. After the Easter egg hunt was finished, we just sat around for the rest of the day, eating chocolate, and watching television. I spent some time on social media, which was a big mistake and only made my day seem small and stupid. All of the people that I had incited over to join us for brunch and the Easter egg hunt, all those people who declined my invitation, actually did have other plans. They had all gotten together for a barbecue, up at the Telegraph Station, and to join in on the local council giant Easter egg hunt. The photographs that they shared on social media were all very pretty, they had obviously had a wonderful time, they all looked gorgeous and relaxed, and had wide, beaming smiles in all of the posts. I closed the page down before Ronnie could see, there is no point in making him upset. There was obviously a reason that we were not invited to join them. I wonder if they know just how they chip away at my self-esteem and self-worth?

Alice

Monday 6 April

Dear Diary,

I spent most of the night awake, wondering just why it is that I do not have any friends. Maybe I am introverted? I might appear that way, but that is because I was always taught by my mother not to speak, not to make a fuss, not to have an opinion. I had to learn very early on in life how to lie and how to conceal, her secrets, their secrets, secrets that I didn't want but which I had no way of escaping from. I perfected the art of pretending that everything was fine, that there was nothing in my life of concern. I grew a mask to cover my own face, I have been wearing it for so long, I am not even sure that I would recognise myself if I took it off. The mask is neutral, schooled into a single, unaffected, emotionless expression. Perhaps that is why I have no connection with anyone? Perhaps my mask conveys a lack of interest? It couldn't be further from the truth, what it is actually conveying is an added layer of protection.

Alice

Tuesday 7 April

Dear Diary,

On the very rare occasions that I was allowed to bring a friend from school, they usually took one look at my sister, and then decided that she was the one they wished to align themselves with. Not that I can blame them, she was, I guess, what every person wanted, society's idea of a perfectly normal and modern female. She was outgoing and loud, and she knew how to have a good time. She wasn't shy, she wasn't quiet, and most importantly of all, she didn't always have her head stuck in a book, buried deep in some fantasy world that didn't exist. She loved to go shopping, she was very good at spending other people's money, of convincing them to spend it on her. She would go into the city to nightclubs and pubs, and always went home each time with a different man. She just had a way of drawing people in, and when she had sucked them dry, she would just move on to somebody else. It isn't that I have never had a friend, well actually, I think it is.

There have been a couple of people over the years who I have thought were friends, but it turned out that it was only one-sided. When Ronnie was young, I met a lady called Donna, whose son was the same as mine. We had quite a lot in common and I was hopeful that we would be friends for life, or at least until our sons started at different schools. She suffered from post-natal depression, and I would often help to look after her son while she attended her appointments and had time off from being a mummy, a concept I never could understand. I would have them over on special occasions, the boys would go to each other's birthday parties, and once a week we would go out for lunch. One day she just stopped calling. No text messages. No messages on social media. Nothing. It was as if she had just vanished. Several months later, I sold an item online, and lo and behold, she was the buyer. I messaged her to let her know that I was thinking about her and to make sure that she was okay. She replied and told me that she was fine, but that she was not interested in renewing our friendship as she found that being my friend was just far too exhausting. Then there was Angela. We had been penpals for almost five years when she suggested that we actually meet, which we did. We hit it off in person so much so that she invited me to her wedding, and although I was nervous, having never been to a wedding before, I accepted her invitation. As it happened, Ronnie fell ill and needed an emergency operation. When I told Angela that I was unable to go to her wedding anymore, she was livid! She suggested that I leave Ronnie at home with my mother, and when I refused, she unfriended me across all social media platforms. Sometimes I look her up on social media, when I am feeling especially down or hating myself, just to see what happened to her. Her dreams came true, she married, had a baby, and is working what is, by all accounts, her dream job. More proof that the problem lies with me, and not anyone else. Oh, it isn't all doom and gloom. I did meet a wonderful woman, Jenny, Ronnie's preschool teacher actually, who befriended me when I wasn't worth knowing. She always had something kind to say to me, and ever so slowly, her words started to make me question if what my mother had been saying my entire life really was true or not. We still keep in touch, and sometimes, on days when my mother is being especially cruel, I like to just sit and imagine what my life would be like if Jenny had been my mother instead.

I can almost feel it, can almost feel what people in loving relationships and families have, and that is what I really envy, feeling warm and sunshiny inside. I have never been anything other than cold and dark inside, my flame of hope long since extinguished.

Alice

Wednesday 8 April

Dear Diary,

I literally have no idea how you are supposed to make friends as an adult, I really don't. There are no crafting groups or women's friendship groups in Alice Springs, and even if there were, they would most likely meet in the evening, when the local buses do not operate, meaning that I would have no way of actually getting there in the first place. When I met my son's godmother, we were working together, and we bonded over our obscure love of vintage toys. Nothing the sort of thing that one can easily slip into conversation. I don't want to try the pubs and bars, as I don't drink, and I am not sure that you could actually meet people in those sorts of places. I did think about the library, but it doesn't really cater to those in my age bracket, it is geared more towards the very young or the very old. Maybe the lack of opportunities is an indication that people my age don't make friends? Maybe it is quite simply too late? Everyone I know who has friends all seems to have met either at school, through work, or through netball, none of which apply to me.

Alice

Thursday 9 April

Dear Diary,

I have been awake for twenty-six hours now, the result of a roster stuff up, another staff member calling in sick, and a wretched case of insomnia. I am so tired I cannot even function properly. My eyes are so heavy, yet they won't stay closed. Too tired to think, too tired to sleep. I succumbed to my reckless fantasies this afternoon, and texted Caleb, a message that was perfectly worded to me, telling him that I like him. I then spent the rest of the afternoon and all evening waiting, so very certain that he would actually reply to me. God, talk about desperate! Naturally, with all the anxiety of waiting, I didn't exactly stick to my resolutions. I had intended to, but when my phone buzzed alerting me to a message that was not from Caleb, I was so disappointed, and I can always start eating healthy tomorrow. It wasn't too bad, I only had one bowl of ice cream, with barely any sprinkles on top. I know, I know. I feel like such a failure already, urgh! In any case, I am now more than ever determined to put this whole Caleb debacle behind me. Starting tomorrow, I'm sticking to my resolutions, I can still make this my best year yet!

Alice

Thursday 16 April

Dear Diary,

On my lunch break, I checked my mobile phone for any text messages, and there was one there from Caleb. I have his phone number programmed into my phone in case he needs to text me any changes to Ronnie's music lessons. I cannot believe that he replied. I just sat there, staring at the screen, not sure what to do. I couldn't breathe I was in such a panic. I had such an ache in my chest, such actual physical pain, but I did the only thing that I thought I could do, and I deleted the text message without reading it. As much as I know that I like him, I am almost as certain that he does not like me, and in that case, I just do not what to know, I do not want to read those words in a text message, it would just tear me apart. No, far better to not know, to always be wondering.

Alice

Sunday 19 April

Dear Diary,

So, my hot water system broke today in spectacular fashion, It just started gushing water off the roof, much to Ronnie's delighted squeals. It is just one more thing that I have to try and find the money to fix. There are days when I wish I had never bought this rubbish house, honestly, there are days when it feels like the biggest mistake of my life. I was just so desperate to have a home for Ronnie, that I overlooked a few issues, issues that are now coming back to haunt me.

Alice

Monday 20 April

Dear Diary,

I can't stop thinking about Caleb's text message, obsessively thinking about what it could have said. I wish I had not deleted it, I wish I knew what he had to say, although I can probably guess. He probably told me to sod off, that he is currently married, or gay, or some other reason. It would be unlikely that someone like him was single. I tried to see if there's a way to recover deleted text messages, but there isn't, or at least if there is, I haven't worked it out yet.

Alice

Thursday 23 April

Dear Diary,

I read an article on the news website today about a twenty-five-year-old man and his seventy-six-year-old lover. He said that it didn't matter what she looked like, that love was what was on the inside, not the outside. God, I wish that were true! She gave an interview on live television in which she told the hosts that he had left her saddle sore and that they had used an entire tube of lubricant their first time! How embarrassing! She loves him, despite her son telling her that he is just after her money, that she ought to be careful. Even if he is just using her for her money or to get himself into the country, you have to admire her conviction. She is determined that he loves her and that is enough for her. That is all anyone really wants, isn't it? To be loved, to be wanted. It is all I have ever wanted; I know that much for sure. Which is what led me to making the biggest mistake of my life, texting Caleb.

Alice

Saturday 25 April

Dear Diary,

I am so lonely; my mind has created within itself the biggest mirage. I am starting to think that perhaps I should give Eric a chance, at least he seems to want to be with me, and maybe that will be enough? I know it is just my loneliness playing tricks with my mind, dressing Eric up as a possible oasis in my life, but the false hope only serves to weigh me down, to drown me faster.

Alice

Thursday 30 April

Dear Diary,

I decided to splurge on flights to the United Kingdom for Ronnie and I for Christmas. We have always wanted to go, and I have the time off work, so what am I waiting for? I may never get another chance to take him. I booked the flights today and surprised him after school. I have no idea where we will stay while there, or what we will do, or anything else, but I am excited to have the tickets. It is real now. Now we can do the fun planning, like work out what we want to see and do. I might even see if I can take Ronnie over to Paris to see the Eiffel Tower, I know there is a train that goes across to France from England.

Alice

MAY

Friday 1 May

Dear Diary,

I am currently sick again, this time it's some kind of strep throat or tonsillitis or something equally gross. I have a doctor's appointment this afternoon after work. Yes, I'm still at work, the last thing I need is to lose my job on top of everything else that I have to manage.

Alice

Saturday 2 May

Dear Diary,

I saw the doctor today and joy oh joy, I have a nasty case of tonsillitis. It is so bad that the doctor has actually referred me to the hospital to have an emergency tonsillectomy! Not sure how long that will take until I'm at the top of the waiting list, even though he marked the request as urgent it could still take a few months.

Alice

Sunday 3 May

Dear Diary,

It has been one thing after another today. Eric will not stop texting me, and it is driving me crazy! Honestly, will he ever learn? Go away and stop bothering me. I had a phone call this morning from the hospital, because of all the rain communities have been having, the roads are flooded, meaning that a lot of patients have not been able to come into town for their surgeries. With a lot of free theatre time, the waiting list has been dramatically shortened, and first thing tomorrow morning, I am going under a general anaesthetic to have my tonsils removed.

Alice

Monday 4 May

Dear Diary,

The operation went well, they did it as day surgery so that I did not need to stay in hospital overnight. I am back at home, tired, in a lot of pain, really, really tired.

Alice

Thursday 7 May

Dear Diary,

I haven't been able to swallow for the last two days. I have been in absolute intense agony; the pain was so bad today that I went up to the emergency department. They had a look in my throat and got the specialist involved and discovered that I had a nasty, nasty infection at the site of the operation. They gave me some fluid and some pain medication through the intravenous drip, which did seem to help, and they sent me home with really heavy-duty pain medication. I won't be able to sleep because it's a steroid-based painkiller, but I will be able to swallow which will be a blessing.

Alice

Friday 8 May

Dear Diary,

It is Mother's Day this weekend, typically one of the longest days of the year in my house. To be perfectly honest, I would do away with the day altogether, but my mother would never let me hear the end of it. Never mind what I want, never mind what is best for my peace of mind, for my soul, for my mental health. It would be different, if I had actually had a proper mother, instead of a biological one only. It would be different if I myself had people around me who felt that I was worth celebrating as a mother, who thought I was worth celebrating at all. The reality is that I don't. I am on my own. Just Ronnie and I. If I were to die, Ronnie would have nowhere to go but into state care. It is a thought that keeps me awake at night, but that is the reality of my life. I have no one, I don't even have anyone to put down on forms as a next of kin contact for myself. I wonder if people who have family members and friends realise just how very lucky they are? They probably can't imagine, not even for one second, that there are actually people who literally have no one in their life. I know whenever I have to fill in forms people are always surprised when I have no next of kin. They always suggest I use a family member, when I tell them that I have no family, they suggest a friend. When I tell them that I have no friends either, they brush it off, assuring me I can leave it blank if I want to, raising their eyebrows, as if convinced that I am lying. If only I were.

Alice

Saturday 9 May

Dear Diary,

Every day I am with her, every day I allow her to take up residence in my home, in my life, I learn to hate myself a little bit more. Nothing I ever do is good enough, her voice echoes in my head. I am just too. Too fat. Too stupid. Too ugly. Too much. Too everything for anyone to ever want to love me. Her words, not mine. Forty years I have endured abuse and trauma at her hands, at her words, at her actions. How much longer must I go on? No one to tell, she made sure of that, whispering behind my back, mentally impaired is what she used to say to people who wanted to be friends, until, at last, they all went away. Day into night, night into day, forty years wishing my life away. I'll die before

I ever live, she will make sure of that. My rage, my hatred for her grows every day, under the surface, just bubbling away.

People think I am so lucky, to have my mother around. Does it make her feel good? To know that her lies are so sound. No one to help me, no one to care, I wish I just had one person with which to share.

Alice

Sunday 10 May

Dear Diary,

Another long, tiring, exhausting, day. All I want, all I have ever wanted since becoming a mum, is to have a single mother's day where I am loved and spoilt. All I want is to be celebrated. Is that really too much to ask for, to hope for? My mother seems to think so, she is always telling me that there is no reason why I should be treated like a princess, that it is not as if Ronnie knows what mother's day is anyway, and even if he did, it wouldn't be something he cared that much about. My mother is such a hurtful cow. She knows how achingly desperate I am to be loved, how very starved I am of any form of affection. She knows how deeply I love Ronnie; she knows that he is the only person I have ever loved, that I would die for him, that every single decision I make is for him and because of him. I was born to be his mum, and my mother knows this, that is why she takes every opportunity to belittle me and to trash my skills as a mum, because she knows how very deeply it hurts me. She's wrong, though, Ronnie does know what mother's day is, he knows how upset it makes me, and he is always more snuggly and quieter on this day. I know he is more subdued as he is picking up on my distress, it doesn't help that my mother is always so mean to him as well. She refuses to take him shopping for me, even though I pay for the gift and give her a list of things that I would like. I just can't face shopping for myself, choosing the wrapping and the card, wrapping everything up and then acting surprised when I open it, it is just do depressing. When Ronnie was in year one, I begged and begged, and finally convinced my mother to take Ronnie shopping for a gift for me for mother's day. I gave them one hundred dollars, and a list of gift ideas, which included things like a hardcover novel, my favourite chocolates, a new handbag, and other bits and pieces. Ronnie was annoyed when they got home from shopping, but he wouldn't tell me why. My mother brushed aside my concerns, assuring me that Ronnie had chosen what he wanted and that I should just leave well enough alone. So, I did. Then, I made a fatal error. I got my hopes up. When mother's day dawned, Ronnie looked less than impressed when he handed my gifts over, and I just knew, that there would be something wrong. There were two gifts in total, one big, one small. I opened the big one first to discover, to my horror, a robotic vacuum cleaner. I don't even have carpets. I was flooded with disappointment, struggling to find something, anything, nice to say about the gift, stumbling over my words as my mother sat there and grinned a smug little grin. She knew I hated it, knew I had no need of it, knew what had been on my wish list. The second, smaller, gift, was opened with trepidation, slowly. With the wrapping finally free, the gift was revealed to be a miniature torch, for what purpose exactly no one was able to tell me. I didn't even get a card. I couldn't even pretend to like it, so bitter was my pain, bile rising in my throat. I excused myself on the premise of having a shower, standing under the water as the tears poured from my eyes. I no longer ask my mother to take Ronnie shopping for me. I no longer shop for myself, so farking tired of everything, I now just don't bother celebrating mother's day for myself at all. Oh, we still celebrate it for my mother, make no mistake about that, if she wasn't pampered and waited on hand and foot Ronnie and I would never hear the end of it, not that anything we ever do is good enough for her mind you. It makes for an exhausting day, emotionally, pretending not to care that you are not celebrated as a mother, all the while bending over backwards to please your own mother, whom you don't even like, let alone love. There are so many landmines to navigate in my house on mother's day, I wonder if anyone else avoids mother's day? Ronnie and I cook breakfast for my mother, usually pancakes or something else that she chooses, despite no one else eating them. Lunch is always a roast lamb, never cooked to her liking no matter how it is done. Dessert is pavlova or trifle that she eats straight from the bowl with a spoon. We buy her chocolates every year, and then she points out what gift she wants as we are out and about in town in the weeks leading up to mother's day. It is never enough though. Last year she wanted a new handbag, leather, which I bought despite the cost, in order to keep the peace. The bag was fine, but she was miffed there was no matching wallet. Keeping a person happy, keeping the peace to avoid a mental health mood swing, is hard work, more so when you don't even like the person. One day, god willing, when my mother is dead, Ronnie and I shall have our first mother's day. I already know exactly what my ideal, my perfect, mother's day would be. It would be the same as my ideal, my perfect, birthday. There would be a tablecloth and fresh carnations, homegrown, or store-bought, on the kitchen table when I got up in the morning. Ronnie would greet me with a hug and a kiss, and a happy mother's day, and then the two of us would sit at the table and have our morning coffee together. We would cook breakfast together, it would be our favourite, a full

English, complete with toast, oven-cooked bacon, chipolatas, scrambled eggs, and baked beans. After breakfast we would do something together, a wander around the farmer markets, or the trash and treasure markets, before coming home to organise lunch, roast beef with roast potatoes, roast butternut pumpkin with the skin on, gravy, and dinner rolls with butter curls. The afternoon would see us playing a board game or cards together, or maybe watching one of our favourite movies together. Dinner would be leftover roast meat and gravy sandwiches, followed by a dessert of chocolate mousse. The entire day would be about togetherness and love, the activities, and meals we shared would be things that we both enjoy doing together, foods that we both love. I can see it all in my mind, my perfect day spent with my precious Ronnie.

It is this created memory that keeps me going on the hard celebration days where I am forgotten, swept to the side, neglected.

Alice

Monday 11 May

Dear Diary,

I really wish that I had had a mother, a proper, loving, nurturing, mother. I often think that if I had had a real mother, even for a short time, that it might have altered the entire trajectory of my life. Sometimes I imagine what my real mother, my soul mother, might be like. She would have loved me, even before she had met me, she would have loved me from the very first moment that she thought of bringing me into the world. She would have had a life that she loved, her family would have brought her immense joy. She would have been there to wave me off to school in the morning, and there to welcome me home in the afternoons. When I was sick, she would have taken me to the doctor, would have fussed over me and nursed me. She wouldn't have left me to fend for myself, ever. She would never have teased me or belittled me. She would never have compared me to my siblings or encouraged us to compete for her affections. She would have listened, to me, to my dreams, without judgement or ridicule. She would have supported me, no matter what I wanted to do, no matter how outrageous it seemed to her. She would have loved me. She would have supported me, emotionally, she would have been my biggest cheerleader. She would have celebrated me and my life, she would have made me a birthday cake, she would have made me feel special, even on those days when I felt anything but. She would not have made fun of me. She would not have teased me. She would have taught me to love myself, not to hate myself. I would never have doubted her love for me. She would have seen that I was equipped with the skills needed to succeed in this cruel world, of that I am certain. Do you think that such a mother actually exists? Or is it just a wonderful type of daydream, like winning the lotto? If such a mother really exists, her children must feel so blessed, so special. I hope they realise just how very lucky they actually are, I hope they realise that people like me, families like mine, exist.

Not that I would call my mother and I a family, more like forced flatmates. I have so much pain and truth locked inside, buried deep, hiding, not just from me, but from the rest of the world as well. I am so tired, tired of pretending that everything is fine, tired of always fighting to be seen, to be heard, just tired of life.

Alice

Tuesday 12 May

Dear Diary,

There are days when I am so grateful for my love of reading, for my ability to appear fully immersed in a paper world. I can manage, for a short time anyway, to block out the voices around me, the nasty comments and hurtful slurs. It's amazing what people think they are allowed to say in order to get someone's attention when they are reading. I have schooled my mask face well, I no longer display any emotions in public, the only time I allow myself to feel is when Ronnie is asleep and I am safe in bed, in the dark, fist in my mouth to stifle my sobs. My only friends, my constant companions, are the voices in my head, my imaginary friends, characters from books read and movies seen. People who can't hurt me and who will never leave me.

Alice

Wednesday 13 May

Dear Diary,

I was eighteen the first time I tried to kill myself. It was surprisingly simple really. I merely made an appointment for the local general practitioner doctor and told him I was unable to sleep, he prescribed sleeping pills without question. The more doctors I visited, the more pills I managed to amass. It didn't work though, I didn't take enough, and instead of dying I merely felt very, very, ill. I remember waking up in the emergency department of the local hospital, being told to drink a cup full of a charcoal solution, foul-tasting gunk. Once the nurse had turned away, I poured the entire contents into my handbag, claiming that I had in fact drunk it. she believed me and I was discharged. The second time I attempted to kill myself, by the same means, they watched me as I drank the charcoal solution. I was then admitted into the psychiatric hospital for three days. It wasn't until the third day that I saw a doctor, up until then I had merely stayed in bed watching television and napping. The doctor was male, middle-aged, white, privileged. There was no consult, no clinicians room. He merely walked up to me in the hallway as I sat near a window, introduced himself, and then told me that had spoken with my mother and he thought that I was being incredibly selfish and that I should start thinking about my family. I didn't tell him that it was in fact my mother that was the sole reason for me wanting to die, that I could no longer endure the horrid abuse, the trauma that came from her hands. I didn't tell him that only a week earlier, the day after my eighteenth birthday, I had agreed to go to a flea market with my mother in order to keep the peace. If I had refused I would never had heard the end of how I never want to do anything, how I never want to socialise, how I cost her the bargain of the century and so on. I didn't tell him that while we were at the flea market, I stopped to look at some containers, only to glance up and find my mother gone. After wandering around for a while I headed back to the car where I found her sulking. On and on she went, her voice growing louder and louder, not caring that she was drawing attention to us, not caring that people were now pointing at us. How dare I go to look at the containers, she had wanted to look at books, why couldn't I just be normal? Why couldn't I be more like my siblings? Why couldn't I just do what she wanted for a change? I got into the car and she sped off down the highway, raging all the way. About halfway home she fired her kill shot, telling me that I was the biggest disappointment in her life, that she regretted ever keeping me. Just let that sink in. My mother told me that I was the biggest disappointment in her life, that she regretted ever keeping me. My mother. And she wonders why I loathe my life, myself, why I pray that I would just die, that my life, my misery, would end. I didn't tell the doctor this, I daresay he would have thought her justified. Although the doctor didn't cure me of my suicidal tendencies, he did do two things for me. Firstly, he made me realise that no one, not even doctors, care, that when it comes down to it, all you have is yourself, and that it is a complete waste of time trying to talk to a doctor, they don't want to know, they don't want to listen. Secondly, I vowed that next time I try to kill myself, and there will be a next time, that I will do it right, there will be no mismeasuring or miscalculating of the number of pills needed.

Alice

Thursday 14 May

Dear Diary,

My wayward brother arrived in town today. He just texted my mother to tell her that he was here, apparently, he drove from Victoria to the Northern Territory, on a whim. She has, naturally, gone into town to see him. No idea where he is staying, and I don't care. The last time I saw my brother he was high off his face on drugs, and he tried to throw me off a second storey balcony, all for suggesting that he leave his three-month-old daughter with me for a few weeks while he got himself sorted out. As it happened, he was arrested, an apprehended violence order issued, and his daughter was taken by the department of families and given to her mother's mum for six months.

Alice

Friday 15 May

Dear Diary,

I don't think that I will get much sleep tonight. My brother is essentially homeless, not having put any thought into where he was going to stay while in Alice Springs before he embarked on this crazy trip. He has assured me that he is off the drugs, although I am not entirely sure that I believe him. I have agreed to let him stay here until Monday morning, when he is expected to go and find somewhere else to live. I have put him into Ronnie's room, and Ronnie is in my bed. I am on a mattress behind my bedroom door, I know all too well just how my brother likes to creep into my bed in the night, knife held tightly in his hand as insurance, a guarantee of silence. At least if I sleep behind the door it means that there is no way he can open it and get to me or to Ronnie.

Alice

Saturday 16 May

Dear Diary,

My mother and my brother went out all day today, thank heavens, so I didn't have to make sure Ronnie and I were on high alert all day. Another night behind the door, this time I have my own knife, hiding on a shelf where Ronnie can't reach it, but I can if need be.

Alice

Sunday 17 May

Dear Diary,

My brother woke with a nasty cough, my mother took him up to the emergency department to see a doctor. He is now in the intensive care unit in an induced coma. His years of drug use have weakened his heart so badly that his cold could be deadly. Is it horrible that I don't feel anything? That I am looking forward to being able to sleep in my own bed again?

Alice

Monday 18 May

Dear Diary,

Today the local hospital decided to send my brother down to Adelaide on the Royal Flying Doctor Service aircraft. He is still in an induced coma, and they don't know how long he will be down there, but either way, it has no impact on myself, my life, or anything else really.

Alice

Tuesday 19 May

Dear Diary,

Today my mother got permission to fly down to Adelaide on a commercial airline to be with my brother while he is in intensive care. The hospital transportation service will pay for the airfares which is good, because there's no way that I could afford to do that, and even if I did have the spare money, I certainly would not be spending it on my mother. And no way could I lend it to her, I learnt the hard way that she never pays the money back, conveniently forgetting that money was loaned and not given, besides, she hasn't worked in years so would have no way to pay it back.

Alice

Wednesday 20 May

Dear Diary,

More boring, mundane text messages from Eric. I really have no idea what to do about it, he just does not seem to listen when I speak. I told him not to message me, I told him to go away, that I am not interested, and everything is fine for a day or 2two, and then the messages start again. I don't want to put him offside by being a complete cow to him, as part of me thinks that maybe he is just really lonely, and as somebody who has been alone, and lonely, for thirty-odd years, I know how that can eat away at your soul, I know how that can slowly erode the very foundation of who you are.

Alice

Thursday 21 May

Dear Diary,

My mother phoned me today to let me know that my brother is out of his coma and that the doctors think he will make a fairly quick recovery. They are looking to have him flown back to Alice Springs as soon as possible, maybe even later today if the Royal Flying Doctor Service has an aircraft coming back to base.

Alice

Friday 22 May

Dear Diary,

My brother flew back into Alice Springs early today and will be remaining in hospital for a few days yet.

Alice

Saturday 23 May

Dear Diary,

My brother has been downgraded from serious to stable and is now out of intensive care and into a bed in a general ward. Having him in town has had an unexpected side effect, my mother has been spending every waking moment with him, he has always been undeniably her favourite child, which has meant that Ronnie and I are getting a bit of a break from having her around all the time, which has been pure joy!

Alice

Sunday 24 May

Dear Diary,

My brother is out of the hospital, he has gone into a flat paid for by a local men's shelter. The only stipulation is that he is only allowed to stay there for a maximum of eight weeks, it is essentially a halfway house.

Alice

Monday 25 May

Dear Diary,

It was my brother's birthday today, so my mother made him a cake, and Ronnie and I went with her to deliver it. My brother lives in a pigsty, I nearly vomited when I saw the state of the place. Rotting meat in the fridge, maggots on food on plates in the sink. Disgusting!

We had cake, Ronnie sitting on my knee so that he did not have to sit near my brother, all while listening to my brother lament the fact that he is so weak from his heart condition that he can't do much of anything, a shower exhausts him, housework tires him out, he can't even wank as he has no energy. Way more information than I needed or wanted to know.

Alice

JUNE

Monday 1 June

Dear Diary,

When I got home today, my mother went to open the driveway gate, and it got stuck. Instead of trying to find out why it was stuck, she simply yanked on it as hard as she could, and the entire gate snapped off its hinge. I simply shut it and padlocked it. As my house is on a double block, I do have a second driveway, but it doesn't have a carport over it, regardless, it is where my mother will need to park now if she wants to get her car off the street. My mother was going on and on, having a good whinge about the fact that the gate is broken, asking when I was going to get it fixed, and so on. I just looked at her and shook my head, I have absolutely no intention of getting that gate fixed, I don't use that gate, as far as I am concerned, the other one is perfectly fine. I imagine that it will cost quite a few thousand dollars to get that fixed, I don't have that kind of money sitting around, and if I did, I certainly would not be spending it on fixing something that is not an essential item.

Alice

Tuesday 2 June

Dear Diary,

More Eric irritation today. You name it, it happened. Text message, check. Messages on social media, check. An email, check. I'm sure if he could work out how to do it, I would have also had a message written in the sky. It really wears me down. Is this really all I am worth? I should be flattered, I know that. It should flatter me shamelessly, the fact that an actual living breathing human is interested in me. The problem is, of course, that he's not interested in me. What he wants to do to me he could just as easily do to his own hand or to a blow-up doll. He isn't interested in what makes me tick, he doesn't want to know what I like, what I don't like. He sure as heck isn't interested in my hopes or my fears. For that reason alone, his constant bombarding messages make me uncomfortable.

Alice

Wednesday 3 June

Dear Diary,

I met a lady today who is in an arranged marriage.
When she first got married, she was actually in love
with somebody else, but her parents had forbidden the
relationship as he was not a wealthy man. So, it was
arranged that she would marry a stranger, a man whom
she did not love, a man who she did know, a man who
she did not even like, a man from a completely different
country and culture than her own. She moved from her
country hallway around the world to his country once

they were married, far away from all of her family and friends. Her husband had actually gone to her country to find a wife and had met her parents and negotiated the deal. They have now been married for fifteen years and have two children, and when I asked her if she was happy, said that she was. While it is not the life that she would have chosen for herself, she did learn to like her husband, and in time she grew to love him. She does sometimes still think about her ex-boyfriend, the man that she really loved. It got me thinking about arranged marriages. It must be very freeing to marry somebody without the expectation of a romantic passionate love, to just get married and then to spend the rest of your life getting to know each other. See, I am old fashioned, for me, if I were ever lucky enough to marry, it would be for life. I would never divorce, I would be married until my husband or I died, which I know is not a popular notion today. I think the idea of getting married and having the rest of your life to discover each other's quirks is really very appealing and has a lot of merit. I think I could marry for convenience. I think that if they could offer me stability and security, I think that I could grow to like them long term.

Alice

Friday 5 June

Dear Diary,

School holidays start tomorrow, it is hard to believe that it is the middle of the year already, this year seems to have flown past so quickly. It will be nice to have Ronnie home for a while, three weeks of school holidays seems like a nice long break, but the time will fly past. We are going to be staying home, we don't usually go away during school holidays, everything is just far too expensive. I spent the day at work today making a list of all the things I want to do with Ronnie during the school holidays. I make him one every school holiday and he always looks forward to getting it on the last day of term. The list contains practical things for us to do such as go through his wardrobe and make sure all of his clothes still fit and are not worn through, get a haircut, and buy new shoes. The list also includes fun things like having dessert for breakfast, building a cardboard creation, going on a scavenger hunt, staying up until midnight watching movies, and reading a new book or two. The list always includes inside and outside activities, as well as at least one staying up late at night activity, as Ronnie thinks that is special.

Alice

Monday 8 June

Dear Diary,

My brother died today, or maybe last night, nobody's really sure. My mother and he have a standing appointment every morning, they meet in town and have coffee. He didn't show up today. He wasn't answering his telephone, so my mother went to his apartment and there is no answer at the door. She looked through the window and saw his body lying on the carpet in the hallway. She called the police and the ambulance, and when they got there, they broke the door down. He was already dead. I'm not sure how I should be feeling right now. I guess society expects me to be sad. Maybe if we had been a normally functioning family then I would be sad. If I had had a normal brother-sister relationship, if he had been my best friend and confidante, then yes, I guess I would be sad. As it is, the first thing I thought of when I heard the news was thank goodness. Now he can no longer hurt me or torture me. No longer will I have to sleep behind the bedroom door, barricaded in for safety. No longer will I need to be on high alert every second of every day while he is around. No longer will I be paralysed with fear. No longer will I have to be afraid that my deepest, darkest, secrets will be revealed. Is that selfish of me?

Alice

Tuesday 9 June

Dear Diary,

I went with my mother to the funeral home today. I discovered that they do not do cremations in Alice Springs, only burials. For a basic no-frills funeral service and burial, we are looking at around six thousand dollars! I nearly died. Who the hell has that kind of money sitting around? Not me that's for sure. We spent the rest of the afternoon discussing and brainstorming ways in which we might be able to raise the money. My mother considered selling her car. She asked me if I would try and access the equity in my house. I told her I would think about it, but the truth is, I have no equity in this house, and if I did, I would not be trying to access it. I suggested that she start a public funding campaign, the only problem there is that the friends that she has are not very financially flush, nor are they very big on social media, so the sharing of the public funding campaign, and getting the word out, would be quite tricky. Just when we started to discuss the possibility of not actually burying him, of simply leaving him as an unclaimed body in the morgue, which personally I have no issues with, the funeral home called. My biological father has paid for the entire funeral. Probably the only time he's ever done anything for my brother. One can't help but wonder if he would do the same thing for me if I was the one who is dead. Somehow, I doubt it.

Alice

Thursday 11 June

Dear Diary,

The coroner released the body today, so my mother can go ahead and bury him as she planned to on Friday.

Alice

Friday 12 June

Dear Diary,

I always knew that my father was going to be at the funeral, what I didn't realise was that he would be bringing his wife, Margaret, the very woman who destroyed my parents' marriage with her illicit little affair. I also did not realise that my sister would be attending the funeral. Oh, those three looked very nice all together, a little group of rich, selfish, entitled people who know nothing of the struggle of real, actual, everyday people. There's not much one can say about the funeral, or those who attended, it was pretty stock standard. Having said that, I have only been to two funerals, so I don't have much to judge it by. My father looks about the same as the last time I saw him, nearly ten years ago. Maybe a little more grey hair and a little rounded in the stomach area. Margaret looks exactly the same as when I last saw her. I wonder if she's had some work done. Either that or she has exceptionally good genes. Not a grey hair in sight, although I am pretty confident that has more to do with hair dye than with mother nature. As for my sister, she's still the same nasty, selfish cow that she has always been. She has piled on the weight, I guess you can do that when you marry your boss's son, at least that's one way to ensure that she makes partner in the law firm. I stayed out of their way, the couple of people who were there for me and for my mother just raised their eyebrows at the show that my father and my sister put on, whaling, and sobbing as if their hearts were broken, despite not seeing my brother in over eleven years. Afterwards, we came back here, and I bought pizza for everybody, my father and my sister, and Margaret, were not invited. I imagine that they spent the afternoon at the casino, all of them enjoy expensive food and a bit of a gamble.

Alice

Saturday 13 June

Dear Diary,

My relationship with my biological sister has always been fractious. Even as a young child I knew that she was the star of the family. Whatever she wanted, she got, no matter the impact or the sacrifice that anybody else in the family had to make. When she was in primary school, she was in everything, swimming club, gymnastics, netball. If there was ever anything that I wanted to do, I first needed to check if it clashed with something that my sister was doing, and if it did, I couldn't do it because there was no way that my mother would ever have said no to my sister. My mother did everything for my sister. She would make her ball gowns for everything from her primary school graduation to her year ten formal, to her sixteenth birthday party. She would make her fancy cakes for her birthday, she would allow her to have a sleepover or a party just because she wanted them, she would drive her to and from work, or to and from her friends' houses, certainly something that was never even offered to me. Everybody knew that my sister came first, it was just an accepted fact of life. My sister has a very volatile temper and is very easily offended. Sadly, my sister believes that money is more important than anything else in the world. My sister would frequently spend Christmas and birthdays at her friends' houses rather than with her family, this is despite the fact that she was the most spoilt person you have ever met. Every birthday she would give you a list of what she wanted, expensive brand name items, leather bags and pearls, nothing generic, nothing in the middle of the road price range. If you bought something that was not on the list, she simply took it back without a second thought, got the money refunded, and then bought herself something else. I used to be so jealous of her. Everything she ever wanted was given to her without any questions asked. I didn't understand, I still don't understand what that power is that she has. All I knew when I was younger was that she didn't have a single struggle in the world. She had no idea what it was to go without something or to have your dreams and your hopes crushed. As an adult I kind of wish that I had that power. Mind you, not that I would be using it for evil means, but it would be nice to just have people give you what you want, without needing to struggle for everything. When my sister was away at university, she made quite a lot of friends, rich friends. They would go out drinking or shopping nearly every other day, and then my sister would call my mother or I and say that she needed money for the rent, or the food, or for some other bill that she had coming up. After this happened every week for a couple of months, I asked her why she didn't just tell her friends that she could not afford to go out drinking with them. She was mortified! No way was she going to tell her friends she couldn't afford to go drinking, how embarrassing. She would rather live her life in debt than go without. She grew up into a selfish, self-centred, nasty being. She had an apartment once where the owner lived upstairs. She decided that she didn't want to be paying the rent, so she had sex with him instead. Problem solved. She told me that she would never marry, that she was only interested in having sex with somebody if they could give her something in return. Essentially, she became a prostitute. After years of working at a law firm without much growth, she hit the jackpot. She started a relationship with the law firm's owner's son, and that eventually lead to marriage. Her social media posts are all full of the bling-bling that she got, and photos of the exotic destinations they have travelled to. Eventually, she gave him two children, boys, raised by nannies, and everybody seems to be perfectly, blissfully happy. Why is it that nasty people have such an easy life? My sister and I have not spoken in nearly a decade. When I was pregnant, she would call me all the time, asking to borrow money. It makes me so angry when I look back on that time of my life. I was the one who was pregnant, I was the one who was alone, I was the one who wasn't working. She had a full-time job and friends, she had everything. She should have been supporting me. My whole family should have been supporting me. Not financially that's not what I'm suggesting, but emotionally, definitely. Instead, she would call me nearly every week asking if she could borrow money. Stupidly, I would allow her to. I was so desperately lonely, all I wanted was for somebody to talk to. At least if I gave her money, she would call me the following week to ask me for more. When my son was born, she didn't even visit me at the hospital. There were no cards or flowers or gifts. Nothing. A couple of weeks later she wanted us to go to lunch, at a time that suited her, and at a place of her choosing, a licenced seafood restaurant. I don't eat seafood and I don't drink. Regardless, Ronnie and I went. Ronnie was due to be fed, and as I sat at the table breastfeeding him, she told me that it was so disgusting and that I should do it in the toilets. And, because I was so embarrassed and mortified, so ill from having just given birth, and unable to stand up for myself, I did. I sat there in a cubicle and tried to feed him, he was miserable and so was I. He didn't feed, and I ended up going back to the table and sitting there with him on my lap while he cried, and the food my sister insisted that I order, went cold. Eventually, I was able to leave, and Ronnie and I went straight home, where we both ate. A few months later she got a better job offer which she accepted, and she had a party to celebrate. I was not invited of course. When I asked her why that was, she told me that it was because I was a loser single mother and that she did not want me in her life, she did not want to be associated with someone like me. This is despite the fact that her best friend, and mother to her godchildren, not only has five children to five different fathers but is also a heroin addict. With my sister, it is always one rule for her family and one rule for everybody else. We haven't spoken since. To be honest, I don't miss her at all. I certainly don't miss always having to bend over backwards to do everything that she wants, just to please her and to keep the peace.

Alice

Sunday 14 June

Dear Diary,

My father and I have always had a non-existent relationship. When I was thirteen years old, he told me that if I wanted to visit him, I would have to pay for the airfares myself, that as far as he was concerned, he was my biological father only, nothing more. At the time, I was living in Queensland, and he was living in the Northern Territory, so I was never going to be able to afford to pay for an airfare. The same rules did not apply to my brother and sister. When I was sixteen years old, my sister went to visit my father, as did my brother. they were going to spend four weeks with him during the school holidays, and when I rang him to ask if I could go as well, I was told that there was no room. The following day, my brother's best friend came over to the house to ask for my father's phone number. Apparently, my father had told my brother that his friend could come and spend the holidays with him so that he wouldn't be lonely. This is despite the fact that there was no room. It wasn't until my brother and sister returned home and they were unpacking that the truth of the visit was revealed. A photograph shot out of this suitcase. It showed my brother and my sister dressed up all fancy, standing next to my father and my stepmother, in her wedding dress. They had eloped. Without even bothering to tell me. If I had never seen that photograph, I would never have had any idea they were married. That was one of the most hurtful things in my life. I just don't understand it. I mean, am I really such a horrible, awful person? My father never wanted me. I did think once that maybe my mother had had an affair, that maybe, just maybe, my father wasn't actually my father. But that makes no sense. Because both of my parents hated me, both of my parents have always treated me as subpar, as less than my brother and my sister, despite me being the eldest child for both of them. I am so envious of anybody who has a dad, I just cannot imagine how that must feel. What would life look like with a dad? Would they help me with my DIY projects around the house? I honestly don't know, I'm not even sure what it is a dad does. I mean I know what it is that my biological father does, but even I know that that is not what a proper father does.

Alice

Monday 15 June

Dear Diary,

I am seriously considering having another baby. I feel that this is it, my now or never. I am so conflicted! On one hand, I am heading towards forty years old, and am still single, if I wait anymore, I will lose my chance. On the other hand, I have already had a baby on my own, and while I don't regret it for a second, it was hard, having no one to support you, and having to do every single thing myself, every single day. It would be nice to have someone in my corner, someone to share the journey with. Which of course, is a whole other set of problems! So much has changed since I had Ronnie, in the World, in medical advancements, in pricing; I am not even sure I could afford to have a baby now, just another thing to consider.

Alice

Tuesday 16 June

Dear Diary,

I am really, really starting to think seriously about having another child. I've been toying with some figures today, trying to work out what costs would be involved. I just wanted to know how much money I would need to save up before falling pregnant, as well as how much money I would need while I was pregnant, and then after delivery. In terms of actually falling pregnant, there is the actual costs of airfares, most likely down to Brisbane city, as well as accommodation while I was there. The donor sperm is free, in Australia, it is illegal to charge for a sperm donation. The In Vitro Fertilisation clinic fees are around five thousand dollars for a single insemination. Given my age, it is possible that the clinic would require pre-screening tests for any abnormalities, which would see that fee increase exponentially. I'm going to think about it a bit longer, I want to be certain that I am doing this because it is something that I want, and that I am not doing it just because Ronnie is growing up and I am starting to feel lonely and left out.

Alice

Wednesday 17 June

Dear Diary,

Another option for me would be to apply to become a foster carer. In Alice Springs, anybody can be a foster carer, it doesn't matter if you're married or not. It would be a way to grow my family, to help children who are in desperate need of some help, and a way for me to feel needed. The major downside is, of course, the fact that if you take in a child how are you going to care for them for six months without coming to care for them? How do you stop yourself from falling in love with them? How do you give them back without knowing what the future holds for them? If they will be safe and cared for? I'm not entirely sure that I could do that. I am, however, going to apply. I think that I will do emergency foster care only to start with, which will just be a couple of nights here and there. That way I can get a feel for whether or not I think I could handle taking a foster child in on a short appointment arrangement without having my heart broken.

Alice

Saturday 20 June

Dear Diary,

I looked into some In Vitro Fertilisation clinics today, to get some information on their waiting lists and requirements. I have decided that if I go ahead with the second round of In Vitro Fertilisation, that I will use the same clinic that I used when I conceived Ronnie. Logistically, I won't be telling anybody that I am doing this, after all, what people don't know they can't ruin.

Alice

Sunday 21 June

Dear Diary,

When I was pregnant with Ronnie, nothing went to plan. It was a planned pregnancy, not a surprise, it wasn't a mistake. My sister was furious! She wanted me to get rid of it. My mother was not at all interested. My auntie wanted to throw me a baby shower, but my mother told her not to bother, that nobody would come if they knew it was for me. To this day I have never been to a baby shower, I have no idea what goes on at one, or if they are fun. I wish that I did know. My mother ruined every piece of joy in my pregnancy. As soon as she knew that I was pregnant, she told every single person that I knew so that I had no one to share my news with firsthand. I really hated her for that. I was sick throughout my entire pregnancy, I had severe morning sickness all day every day for nine months. When my son was finally born, it was an emergency birth. My blood pressure shot through the roof and his heart rate dropped. There was so much blood in the room a nurse told me later that she wasn't sure if either of us would survive. I had three doctors, two anesthesiologists, four medical students, and six nurses present when my son was born. Born at four forty-four in the afternoon, he was resuscitated at birth and whisked off to the special care nursery. By the time they finished patching me up and I got back to the ward, it was one-thirty in the morning, and I had not yet seen my son. The following day I texted everybody to tell them that he had been born. I was in the hospital for three days. I needed four emergency blood transfusions. I had no visitors, no flowers, no gifts, no cards, nothing.

Alice

Thursday 25 June

Dear Diary,

The easiest part of the whole In Vitro Fertilisation process, I think, is choosing a donor. The clinic will courier me over a catalogue of sorts, a bit like a coffee table book, with a photograph of each donor, as well as all the pertinent information, like height, age, weight, medical background, number of successful donations, a family run down, as well as any other information the donor wishes you to have. Then it is simply a case of choosing one that appeals to me. I had hoped to use the same donor as I used when I conceived Ronnie, but that donor is no longer available. He has reached his maximum number of allowed donations. Never mind, no one will ever know that they are not related unless I decide to tell them anyway. The kids will know once they are old enough to understand that they were chosen, that I purposely conceived them, wanted them, planned for them, yearned for them, loved them.

Alice

Friday 26 June

Dear Diary,

I started to make a list of baby names that I like today, it is really starting to become real now, my hopes and desires. Choosing possible names makes the possibility that much more real for me.

My shortlist of possible boy names:

Oscar Alexander

Winter Nathaniel

Joe Samuel

Hunter Xavier

My shortlist of possible girl names:

Amelie Cielo

Ivy Rose

Violet Eden

Alice

Saturday 27 June

Dear Diary,

I had a horrid start to work tonight, so once things had settled down a bit, I started to make a serious list of all the items that I will need if I decide to have another baby. It was quite fun actually, dreaming and hoping, planning for someone who might never be.

Items I will need to buy for a baby

A cot, I especially love white wooden ones.

A bassinet, an old-fashioned cane one with handles that I can beribbon.

A lambswool for the cot/pram/floor.

A baby capsule for the car, the kind that lifts out of the base.

A baby car seat that converts from six months up to eight years.

A cot mobile.

A baby carrier. I honestly don't know how people manage without one.

Linen for the bassinet and cot, with retro or Rockstar themes, like guitars, science beakers, and chemical symbols.

A change table, white wooden if possible.

Clothes, obviously.

Cotton wraps.

A thermometer.

Toys.

Baby bottles, ones with a natural teat, for boiled water to counteract colic.

A baby bouncer, one of the old-fashioned mesh ones, not an automatic lazy one.

A baby bath.

A stroller, one that faces out or in, collapses with a single hand and is super compact for travelling.

Alice

Tuesday 30 June

Dear Diary,

I found out today that I was accepted as a foster carer. So now I am on the list, I have decided to get the spare bedroom done up nicely, but generically, so that it is ready to go when I get a placement. I have a cot, a toddler bed, and a bassinette with a stand, as well as a changing table, which I want to put into the room, also a bookcase for toys, books, and clothes to go on. I thought I would paint the room white and then add accents depending on the child that I get placed with. So, if it's a short-term placement with a little person who likes fairy tales, I can add some princess themed decal stickers. That way it is easily changed for the next placement.

Alice

JULY

Dear Diary,

My whole life, I swore that when I had kids, they would have better than what I had, and they would know that they were loved and wanted and adored, and that I would never cause them to worry or feel unloved or unwanted. I swore that I would never tease them or make fun of them the way my mother tormented me. But I failed. I am a loser. I am stuck in a hell of a life, with no way out. I am tired and unhappy and desperately lonely. I don't think I will ever be happy. And no one understands. People think that all I need to do is get out more and I will be fine. If only! My narcissistic, abusive mother lives in my house. As a young teen, she refused to teach me how to drive, although she taught my siblings. Once I got a job, I had bills to pay and couldn't afford lessons. I still can't afford driving lessons. I probably never will be able to afford them. Even if I could afford to get my licence, I then can't afford to buy a car anyway. So, I can't just get out, I have to plan everything around public transport. Then if I ever do make a friend, my mother verbally runs them down. If I bring them back to my house, she hovers around being rude to them, so that they feel uncomfortable coming over. Friendships fizzle out after that. I have a couple of friends on social media that live interstate, but I can't tell them everything or they would not like me anymore. One friend told me it was too hard to be friends with me, but that if I got my mother to move out, she would be happy to keep being friends. Not that easy. My mother is a narcissist with bipolar. No one wants her. Her other living child has not spoken to her in over eleven years! None of her sisters or brothers keep in touch with her either. I was always her favourite victim and the only one who can't get away. The eldest, the pain I carry is physical, toxic, unbearable for me. If I didn't have my son to look out for, I would have lived on the streets to escape this vicious abuse. I work so hard to make a nice home and provide food, but nothing is good enough. I got home at eight o'clock last night, and my mother had a tantrum because I was too tired to cook fish. So, she threw a chair at me and then used another one to pin me against the wall while she screamed abuse at me. The same stuff I hear every single day. All in front of my son. She loves tormenting me and likes him to see it. She won't even use my name most days, she just calls me 'fat, fatty, fuck' or 'fat slut'. I don't care what she calls me, but it breaks me that she calls me those things in front of my son. Today when I got to work, she wound down the window and screamed out 'good riddance you fat slut fucker', and all these people heard her. I pretended that I didn't care, and just walked into work. I am so tired. I don't sleep, I don't eat. I have no one to talk to except myself, because seriously, who cares. When I am at home, she goes on and on and generally ends all of her rantings with 'I hope you intend to go to your room and stay in there for the whole fucking day you little fucker'. I can't do anything to escape as I have my son. My only real option is this: pack a suitcase, empty my bank account (on a pay week), declare bankruptcy, take my son and my dog and try to hitch to another state to start again. Obviously, the issue then becomes finding a new job, finding a shelter to live in that allows dogs, finding a new school, changing our phone and emails. But what choice is there? Especially when my mother said to me 'you have no idea how many times I have come into your room at night with a knife, or how close I have come to killing you'. I probably have a tumour from all the stress.

Alice

Thursday 2 July

Dear Diary,

I did something a little crazy today, I called one of the social workers at work and asked them if they knew of any places that I could go, to talk, to just sit. I feel that I am going to lose my head, quite seriously, I feel that I am on track to have some kind of major mental break or nervous break or something. I am just exhausted. I am so tired of going through life merely reading water. Something happened to me when I was a child, and it traumatised me. I have never spoken about it, not really, and I need to address it, and lay it to rest if I am going to have any hope of finally forging ahead with the life I have always dreamed of. She offered to see me herself and is happy to fit me in around my shifts, which is nice of her.

Alice

Friday 3 July

Dear Diary,

I was seven years old when it happened, when I died. It started just like any other normal day. It must have been a weekend, as both my mother and my father were with me, in fact, it is one of only three memories that I have of my father and my mother together. We had gone to visit some friends of theirs, a husband-and-wife pastor team that was living and working at a mission in Darwin. I was wearing my brown school sandals, ugly, chunky things they were, and a homemade summer dress, it was pink and white and had three horizontal panels of fabric, with spaghetti straps at the shoulders. It was my favourite dress. I never wore it again. My hair was up in pigtails, and I had pretty pink ribbons in my hair. While the grown-ups sat on the outside verandah enjoying coffee, I played on the rug on the floor. After a while their son came and asked if I would like to go down to the mission playground for a little while, he had some free time before he had to go to work. My parents agreed that it was okay, and we set off, his large strides, my little legs skipping to keep up.

Halfway to the playground, he said that he needed to use a bathroom, and we went over to one of the unused mission houses, to which he had a key in his pocket. I waited in the hallway while he went to the toilet, and when he was done, he asked me if I would like to play a game, it was a game that only very special people were allowed to play. No one had ever called me special before or asked me to play a game with them. I felt special, all warm inside. We went into the bedroom and he told me to just sit on the bed and wait for him to come back, that he would not be long. When he came back, he was carrying a bowl, a round basin similar to the ones used by hospitals to give you a sponge bath. I have no idea why it would be in a mission house. It was full of soapy water; I could see the bubbles and foam on the rim of the bowl. He placed it carefully on the bed and then took his shorts and jocks off, and sat opposite me, his penis lying flat on the bed between us. I had never seen a penis before, I had no idea what it was, or what it did. He told me to hop off the bed and to take my knickers off, and although I felt icky inside, I did as I was told, before climbing back up onto the bed. He pulled me towards him by my ankles, pushing my dress up to my waist and opening my legs outwards. He took a sponge out of the soapy water and touched me with it, down there. I froze. After a while he stopped and gave me the sponge, telling me to touch his penis, guiding my hands up and down, moaning and grunting as I went. He told me it was fun, that it was nice to play games, that I was such a good girl. He told me that I must not tell anyone else, as we can't play games with everyone, only special people. I just sat there, a stupid frozen smile on my face. At some point he took the sponge off me and placed it back in the bowl, rising to his knees, he pushed me down onto the bed. He told me that because I had been such a good little girl, that I got to play an even more special game, a game that only the two of us was allowed to play. He smiled at me then, a normal smile, the same smile he smiled when we went to church or when he said goodbye to people. Then he laid down on top of me, squashing me. All I remember is the pain, such intense pain, down there, and the feeling that I was suffocating, that I could not breathe, it was the same feeling I got if I ran and ran and ran at school. It was not until many years later that I was able to name what he had done to me, that I knew the word for it. Rape. When he was finished, he looked happy and sweaty. He told me not to move, and he went to have a shower. I stayed right where I was, not daring to move, tingling all over. When he came back into the room he picked my knickers up off the floor and helped me to sit up, sliding my legs into the knickers and pulling them up, straightening my dress. He told me I was such a good girl and reminded me not to tell anyone about our game, they would be upset that they weren't allowed to play too. I nodded mutely. He scooped me up and placed me on his shoulders, carrying me back to the house. I still wore my stupid smile, and I stung, down there, all the way home. That morning was the last time I was really alive, the last time I was ever carefree and happy. I have been wearing a stupid smile mask ever since. My mind is always on high alert, always firing, always pumping. I don't trust people easily. I'm scared of being alone. If I am alone in the house, I have to have all of the doors and windows locked up tight, the phone next to me, just in case. For over twenty years, I have felt disgusted, at myself, dirty, unclean. I was able, for a short while, to stuff the memory of what happened to me deep down inside, locking it away for years, but the feeling of hatred, of revulsion, at myself, remained. Over the years I have learnt all of the facts, that children who are abused are more likely to be abused as an adult, in fact, some studies suggest it is five times more likely. I have never felt safe. Taught to be quiet, I have always been alone in the world, I feel as if I exist on a completely different axis to everyone else. As if I am not really here, like I am looking through a foggy mirror at everyone else getting on with their lives. I became invisible. The night it happened, I told my mother that he had touched me, and gestured to my knickers. My mother slapped my hands away in disgust. She told me that I was being ridiculous, that my lies could get people into trouble. She ridiculed me, mocked me, goaded me, called me stupid for daring to suggest that anyone would ever want to touch me down there. Her tone was incredulous as she spoke. Her reaction tightened the mask on my face. I never spoke of the attack again, and she never mentioned it again either. I wondered if I had secretly liked it. Why didn't I scream? It was not until high school science class that I learnt of the freeze response, putting the well-known fight or flight response on hold, and trapping a victim on the spot. It is more prevalent in children as they are more defenceless. I know this happened. My smile froze and my brain was stopped working. This happened. I wear the same stupid smile mask to this day. It is my only defence. I wear it all day, every single day. It protects me from letting others see just how much they hurt me. If I react, if I feel something, I can't be sure of just what will come tearing out, if I start talking, or crying, or screaming, I may never stop. Over the years people have told me that I am kind, caring, and generous. I don't believe them. How can someone like me, someone who is broken, be anything other than ugly and disfigured? I put on my mask of indifference and nonchalance as soon as I wake in the morning, I wear my mask at all times, just as a wear clothes. Occasionally it slips, I'm not heartless. Just as with my clothes, I take it off when I shower, in the privacy of the water sluicing over my skin, I can be myself, ugly, horrible, black scars and all. In the shower, I can let the loathing and shame have free rein, where no one can hear me cry. The scars on my forearms remind me of my secret shame every single day. Faint scars now, faded over time, but they are there is you know where to look, scars that were self-inflicted in an effort to cope with the anguish and pain, the deep-seated self-hatred and despair that never left me. My anguish was so prolonged, manifesting itself as physical pain, a tightening of my chest, a crook in my neck, that I would have done anything to escape. Compounding my distress was the continued and never-ending torment and abuse that I suffered on a daily basis at the hands of my parents. Abuse that I can't talk about. Abuse that is so uncommon, no one would believe me. The social worker was right about one thing, writing down my rape in my words, owning it, even if it is just on paper, is the first step. I can feel the start of a weight being lifted off me, I can feel my stomach starting to unclench. Writing about my rape, reliving the trauma, doesn't increase it, if anything, it diminishes the power my rapist has over me. Saying it out loud gives me some power back, maybe it will help me to be less scared of everything, to find the closure that I desperately need. It might even help me to learn how to be happy again, or at least, a paler version of happy, a pastel shade perhaps? Something less disgusting than what I am now. Every day I have to live with the result of my rape. I see the effect that it has on Ronnie. I see his confusion and fear when I fly into a rage over something as simple as not being able to find where he put the television remote controls or the milk he spills every single day when he has his breakfast cereal and forgets to clean it up. My son is a sensitive soul, a clone of me, I see how he is becoming wary and scared of the world around him, and I hate it, I hate that I have done that to him, I hate the knowledge that I can trace this back to the day that man raped me on a strange bed in a strange room, to the moment my life paused, froze, ended, forever stuck in limbo. I became proficient in hiding my feelings, burying how I felt, in order to please others, in order to provide society with, externally at least, what appeared to be a functioning member of society. At night I cry, when the house is dark and quiet, wrenching sobs into a pillow already soaked with my tears. I cry for who I was, for the version of me forever lost, for the person who I might have become. I cry for the parts of me that are ruined, the parts of me that yearn for a connection, even though the rest of me knows that it will never be able to happen. I cry for all the dreams I ever had, all of the hopes I once nurtured. I cry for all of the lonely years I have already endured, as well as for all of the ones that are left stretching before me. Mostly I cry for Ronnie, and for the impact that this might end up having on him. I cry for all the things that are wrong with me, for the loser that I am, for the disgusting blackness that lives within. There are no winners in my life, just an emptiness, engulfing me, surrounding me. I have lived in the wasteland for twenty-eight years now, treading water, holding my breath so that I don't drown.

Alice

Sunday 5 July

Dear Diary,

It may have been a mistake to start writing about my traumas, I have done nothing all weekend but replay them and think about them. I spent the weekend mostly in bed, snuggled up with Ronnie, watching television. I am bone-weary.

Alice

Monday 6 July

Dear Diary,

Shortly after I was raped, but just before my parents called time on their marriage, my father had another one of his affairs. My mother had been rostered on to a night shift and had promised my siblings and I that we could stay up late and watch a movie, they always played a family-friendly movie on a Saturday night when I was growing up. I wonder why they stopped doing that? I wish they would bring it back; I miss those simple values. Just before the movie started, there was a knock on the door, and in walked Margaret, one of my father's students from the class he taught at university. My father sent us all to bed and I was so angry that I was not able to stay up late as my mother had promised. When I got up in the morning, I told my mother that we had missed the movie as my father had

had a friend over, and when my mother asked who it was, I saw no reason to lie. I was seven years old; I had no idea that my father was not supposed to have a female friend over at night while his wife was at work, I had no idea that there was something wrong with that. my mother was furious and confronted my father. My father yelled at her and dragged her outside by her arm and threw her down the front stairs. Living in Darwin at the time, we lived in a cyclone proof house, high up on stilts, accessed by an average flight of stairs. The ground floor of the house housed a granny flat and the laundry. My father then walked calmly down the stairs and dragged my mother back up the stairs by her hair, just to throw her down them again. I watched it unfold through the louvres in the lounge room. At seven years old, I thought that it was my fault, that maybe if I had not told my mother about Margaret that my father would not be so angry. It served as proof, to me, that secrets are dangerous and should be kept safe.

Alice

Tuesday 7 July

Dear Diary,

The emotional abuse that I suffered at the hands of my mother really started to manifest itself around the time of my rape. My mother and father were fighting all of the time, and when they eventually called time on their marriage, my mother was left with three children aged seven, six, and four years old. My mother relocated us from all we knew in the Northern Territory, down to her family in very rural New South Wales, to a town that had fewer residents than my old primary school had students. It essentially meant that despite the court awarding fifty-fifty custody, we had no means of seeing our father unless it was school holidays. Whenever my father tried to telephone, my mother would always find a reason that we needed to end the call early, like it being shower time, or dinner being ready. Whenever my father would send Christmas gifts or items we would need for school, my mother would always make snide remarks about how inappropriate they were, or how useless they were. It really set the tone for the way that we were taught to view our father. After the rape, I began to have toileting issues, and my frequent accidents caused my mother no end of fury. The abuse really ramped up once we were settled into our small new town. My mother had us full time, at her making, and she lashed out in the only way she knew how, with words as sharp as arrows, easily piercing through my thin, vulnerable armour. There was a multitude of physical abuses as well, she once broke a wooden spoon over my backside, but those heal fairly quickly. What doesn't heal, however, are words. They take up residence in a person's very soul, their psyche. They slash and wound a person's heart, seeping in a poison so heinous it is nearly impossible to eradicate. Every new insult, every hurtful slur, is another slash on the heart, another dose of poison. If I were to be cut open, you would find no heart left, just a mass of gaping wounds barely holding together.

Alice

Friday 10 July

Dear Diary,

Perhaps the most hurtful of insults for me, at least as a child, was to be called fat. It was said in such a way as to leave no doubt in my mind that my mother, for whatever reason, considered fat to be something to be ashamed of, something to aspire not to be, at any cost. When I was eight years old, I wanted to sing a song for my mother, and she insisted that my sister sing as well. Then she insisted that we make it a competition, that my sister would sing the song first, and then I would sing the song, and then my mother would decide which of us had sung it better. I was convinced that I would win, it was a song that I adored, almost as much as I adored singing, which, as a young child, I felt confident doing and secure in the knowledge that I was good at it. So off we went, in yet another competition concocted by my mother. After I had finished singing, I turned around eagerly, desperate to hear my mother's verdict. My sister won. How could that be? I contested it, argued with my mother that my sister was out of key. My mother informed me that even if she had been out of key, it was still nicer to watch my sister sing than to watch me sing, that at least my sister hadn't been standing on the lounge, our makeshift stage, waggling her fat arse all over the place. The barb was sharp and successful in its mission. I never sang in the presence of another person again, to this day, I only sing when no one is around to hear me.

Alice

Saturday 11 July

Dear Diary,

My mother's most used catchphrase with me is something that to this day I still hear. I hear it from her lips, I hear the echo of it in my mind, I hear it in my voice when I look in the mirror. Who on earth would ever want someone like you? It was something that my mother trotted out with an alarming frequency. If I commented about getting married one day. Who on earth would ever want someone like you? If I spoke of wanting to have children. Who on earth would ever want someone like you? If I spoke of my dream occupation. Who on earth would ever want someone like you? It was easily interchanged with the phrase who on earth would ever love someone like you? I would hear it said to me, never to my siblings, several times a day, sometimes several times an hour. Every single time my mother said it to me, in her condescending, sneering voice, I hated her a little bit more. Every time it was said, it destroyed me a little bit more inside. It crumbled my heart, my hopes, my dreams. The very thing I hated became a self-fulfilling prophecy. No one ever asked me out on a date, no man has ever spoken to me or flirted with me, therefore it must, logically, be true. Who on earth would ever want someone like me? Who on earth would ever love someone like me? It turns out that the answer to those questions is quite simply no one, nobody, not a single soul.

Alice

Sunday 12 July

Dear Diary,

When I was nine years old, I was invited to a sleepover at a classmate's house. It was my first sleepover, the only sleepover I have ever been invited to. My mother gave me permission to go, and I excitedly waited for the big day, desperate to go, to make friends, to fit in somewhere. My mother walked me over to the house, the girls that had already arrived were playing, taking it in turns to sit in a tractor tyre while an adult pushed it around the garden. It looked like so much fun and I ran over to join them. My mother shouted across the yard to the adult, telling them not to let me have a turn, that I was not to be trusted, that I would most likely wet my knickers. My mask froze in place, I pretended that I didn't hear her, that I didn't see the girls look at each other, and when they laughed, I laughed too, pretending that I was in on the joke, instead of being the joke. I don't remember much about the sleepover after that, I imagine that we ate food and played games, but I do vividly remember bedtime. The lounge room had been filled with mattresses and camping beds, and I was sitting in a recliner chair. There was a movie playing on the television. The girls all around me were talking, my eyes were so heavy, I just wanted to shut them for a moment. I heard one of the girls laughing, teasing that I would be the first one to go to sleep. She was right. When I opened my eyes, it was morning. The girl who had invited me, I can't remember her name now, never spoke to me again. I just kept wearing my mask at school, pretending that it didn't matter.

Alice

Monday 13 July

Dear Diary,

Is it useful, to relive memories? I am not sure. On one hand, it does seem to be having a cathartic effect on me, even if I am just writing them down, essentially telling myself what I already know, I feel like I am putting it out there into the universe, and that in itself is powerful. On the other hand, I feel tired, ripped open, raw. I am over analysing everything, second-guessing myself. Laying my trauma bare on the page in black and white has made me see just how horrid my current situation is, just how unhappy I really am, and for how long. It has thrown my job, and the racism directed at me by my colleagues, into stark light. I cannot afford to be without a job, but I am not comfortable with staying put there anymore, with remaining silent.

Alice

Wednesday 15 July

Dear Diary,

It was not just at my mother's hand that I
experienced abuse. My sister would frequently belittle
me in front of her friends, they seemed to find it a great
sport. They would have no issue with commenting
about the way my clothes fit, how ratty my clothes
looked, or my intelligence. My sister even went as far
as to use me as an example in one of her university
assignments, about socialisation and the curse of the
modern loser. My mother read it and thought it was
fantastic.

Alice

Thursday 16 July

Dear Diary,

It is hard to believe that I used to be a size fourteen! I am now a size twenty. A huge, blubbery, revolting, mass of a human being. I can only imagine how much my weight embarrasses Ronnie. I am so full of shame over the way that I look. I know that I am an emotional eater, I always have been. I found comfort in food, comfort that I got nowhere else. Food didn't abuse or mock me. When I was thirteen, my mother would constantly tell me that I should be trying to lose weight not put more on or tell me that I didn't need to buy whatever food item it was that I had put up on the checkout at the supermarket. The more I loathed her, the more I turned to food for solace, the more I relied on food to help me after a bad day. I don't know how to undo that way of thinking.

Alice

Monday 20 July

Dear Diary,

When I was nineteen, my sister hosted an underwear party, essentially a way to buy underwear through a party plan scenario. There was a pretty top that the presenter needed a model for, and my sister nominated me. I was stupidly flattered, I thought that she was genuinely reaching out to me, trying to build a bridge. No. when I came out of the bathroom having changed into the top, every single one of the guests laughed. At me. My sister stood up and commented that now we have all seen how not to wear a top, that she would show everyone how to wear it properly, seeing as how she wasn't too fat to wear it. Face flaming, I got changed, then sat through the rest of the party without uttering a single word. Despite feeling pretty in a couple of the pieces, I didn't order anything. To this day, I don't try clothes on in a shop, I just buy a size twenty or twenty-two, whatever they have, and take it home. Most of my clothes are too baggy, done by choice. I don't ever want to be called fat in front of a group again, I don't want people laughing at me because they think my clothes are too tight. It had such an impact on me, I don't even go into clothes shops. I shop at thrift stores or buy what I need from online auction sites, I have never spent any serious money on clothes, I have never felt good in anything I have ever worn. Ugly inside and ugly outside, why put in any effort?

Alice

Tuesday 21 July

Dear Diary,

The issue with trying to address past traumas and abuses is that you start to see everything else wrong in your life!

Alice

Wednesday 29 July

Dear Diary,

Work has been so draining this month, which I know has more to do with me and my emotional state than with the actual workload.

Alice

Thursday 30 July

Dear Diary,

I am so glad that this month is over, it has been emotionally very hard for me. Sometimes I wonder if I am the only person who thinks that their brain is broken. When I am alone, I talk out loud to imaginary people. I know they don't exist, I'm not crazy, I know I am the only person in the room, but I still talk out loud to them, nonetheless. This is how lonely I am.

Alice

AUGUST

Monday 3 August

Dear Diary,

I was culling my social media posts and presence today, and there was a message in one of my spam folders, an invitation actually, to my high school reunion. It has been twenty years since I was last inside that school, not sure that I have any desire to go back and relive anything. Besides, I have always thought that reunions were really just for the students who had friends at the school, not for loners like myself. I went to delete the message, and then I felt bad. Someone had gone to the effort of tracking me down in order to send me that invite, I should at least have the decency to reply and tell them that I won't be attending. Right? I just closed the page down; I will think about how best to write my non-attendance reply later in the week.

Alice

Tuesday 4 August

Dear Diary,

In retrospect, my entire school life can be summed up by a papercut. So incredibly painful, and invisible. By the time I reached high school, I was painfully introverted, agonisingly shy. I would never have spoken up for myself, never have spoken unless asked a direct question. My mother had relocated my family from New South Wales up to Queensland a couple of months before high school was due to start, meaning that unlike the rest of my year cohort, I was not coming from a local primary school, where I had friends and people that I knew, I was coming from a completely different state. It didn't help matters that my mother refused to buy me a uniform that fitted, instead, after purchasing new items for my sister and my brother at their respective schools, took me down to the uniform shop with fifty dollars and told the uniform shop assistant that I would need as many second-hand clothes as possible, including textbooks, as my mother refused to pay more than she had to for me. The shop assistant told my mother that they didn't have any items in my size, they only had second-hand items as they were donated, so my mother simply got the sizes that they had available. I can still remember having to wear a skirt that, despite my mother being able to sew, dropped down to my ankles instead of being the required knee length; and the shame of trying to keep my too small blouse buttoned over my large chest.

Alice

Wednesday 5 August

Dear Diary,

I spent most of the first term of high school paralysed with anxiety. My mornings were full of tears, and shamefully begging my mother to allow me to stay home, not to force me to go to school. This would be followed by me dragging my feet on the walk to school, trying not to cry the closer I got, hoping that no one would notice me yet praying that someone would ask if they could be my friend. The subjects were not an issue, I have always had a very high intelligence, and easily topped all of my classes. That first term though, every recess and lunchtime would find me sitting in the counsellor's office, not wanting to go out to where the other kids were all sitting in groups, wanting to hideaway.

Alice

Thursday 6 August

Dear Diary,

It really is no surprise that I was bullied at school, I was the perfect target. I came from a single-mother household, and we were poor. I don't mean poor as in we only have one television, I mean poor as in we had no television, and every day we had a choice to make, we could either have breakfast or we could have lunch, but there was never enough food in the house to have both. So, then you get the poor, fat kid, with no food, no friends, nothing. I wore thick glasses, and everyone knew me as the kid who only had one expression for everything. As far as targets go, they don't get much better.

Alice

Friday 7 August

Dear Diary,

By far my worst school memory, the very worst, was the time that I wet my pants in front of the whole school. I was thirteen. It was my first day at the local high school, my mother had not taken me down the week before for orientation, and as I was new to the area, I had no friends with which to sit with. I had managed to find my homeroom, and most of my classes that first day, and I had found a bit of shade in which to sit and eat my sandwich for lunch, but by the end of the day I still had not seen a bathroom, and by now I had a desperate need to use one. All of the homerooms had been assembled in the school hall for a roll call before the final period. As I was sitting there, by myself, surrounded by groups of chattering friends, I knew that I could no longer wait to go to the bathroom. I tried to get up to ask a teacher for directions, a scary prospect for a shy introvert like myself, but my leg had gone numb while I had been sitting on the hall floor, and until the pins and needles started to set in, I was unable to move. As much as I tried to hold it, I could not, and I started to wet myself. I was so humiliated! I started crying, I went bright red, and when the teacher asked me what was wrong, I couldn't speak. She made me stand up, at which point it became obvious as to why I was crying. All the other kids in the homeroom started to snigger, and the teacher called another student over to take me up to the counsellor's office. We walked in complete silence. The counsellor found me a lender uniform, and my mother was called. She was furious when she collected me, yelling at me without pause. For weeks afterwards, she took great delight in telling everybody just how disgusting her daughter was.

Alice

Sunday 9 August

Dear Diary,

One of my co-workers came in today with the most wonderfully coloured hair. It looked so pretty, shiny, and flowy, a riot of rainbow colours. I asked her if she had done it herself and the whole office erupted in laughter. She corrected me coldly, it had been done at a local salon and had cost her a small fortune. My stupid gaffe sparked a conversation that lasted for the rest of the shift, about hairdressers and hair routines that everyone has. I kept quiet, I had nothing to contribute to the conversation. I cut my own hair using an electric razor, actually the same one I use for trimming the dog's hair, a hairdresser being well out of my budget. Somehow, I don't think that a daily shampoo counts as a routine. I hate my hair, always have. As a child, my mother would never allow me to wear it how I wanted to. I wanted to grow it long, like my sister, but instead, it was cut into a bob style. The only thing that ever went into my hair was yoghurt, and that was not my choice. When I was at high school, the boys, those gorgeous, heart-stopping, unknown creatures, used to take it in turns to see who could throw their yoghurt, a surprisingly popular lunchbox snack in the late nineties, into my hair. Most of them were terrible shots, but one day, as I sat there by myself, pretending to enjoy my sandwich with the incredibly stale bread, there was a sickening splat sound and a thump to the back of my head. A full tub of strawberry yoghurt had landed fair and square on the back of my head and was dripping down my neck. I pressed my lips together and hoped I wouldn't cry. The guidance counsellor was kind enough to scrape it all out for me, I never mentioned how it had happened, and the boys never did it again.

Alice

Tuesday 11 August

Dear Diary,

By some stroke of luck, I was rostered off today, which was a nice surprise. With Ronnie at school, I actually did something that I have not had time to do for ages, I read a book. I adore reading, it quite literally saved my life, many times over. While I was growing up, books were my solace, my only friends. The worlds and places I visited inside those pages were real to me, the people and characters, my family. Once I started high school, I turned even more towards books. After the whole yoghurt incident, I no longer took lunch to school and instead, once the bell rang, would go straight to the library, and hide myself away between the shelves. It was the only thing that got me through those horrid years.

Alice

Wednesday 12 August

Dear Diary,

I am on the night shift tonight, so am writing this on the sly. One of the day shift staff brought in a box of assorted chocolates and candy bars for a fundraiser, and I am having an internal debate over if I should buy one or not. I'll probably lose. I have never been able to resist a nice chocolate bar or a yummy piece of candy, not since French lessons in high school, what a mess that was! As I was the only student who wanted to study French, I was given a correspondence course to complete, and if there was a teacher free, they would supervise me. Usually, there wasn't, which then meant that I had to go into a storeroom and study there. I'm ashamed to say that when I was in the storeroom, sometimes I would not study so much as I would poke around in the storeroom and see what they had in storage. One day I hit the jackpot. Several boxes leftover from the previous weekend's school fete, the same fete I was never allowed to attend, had been dropped off. No one had had a chance to go through them and sort them out yet, and when I succumbed to curiosity, I found dozens of bags of mixed lollies. To most people, this find would have been nothing spectacular, but to me, to someone who had never had lollies, who didn't even know that half of these types even existed, it was jaw-dropping. I reasoned that they wouldn't miss a single bag, it wasn't as if they could reuse them the following year. I spent that whole lesson sitting there, savouring the taste of every single bite of my stolen bag of lollies. To this day, I love a bag of mixed lollies.

Alice

Friday 14 August

Dear Diary,

After thinking about it, I have decided that I will go to my high school reunion, it might be good to get some closure, to see where all of my peers ended up. Also, it is in Brisbane, so I will be able to have my initial appointment at the In Vitro Fertilisation clinic to start the process, which will be nice.

Alice

Monday 17 August

Dear Diary,

I baked a cake today, for Ronnie's birthday tomorrow. I am really happy with how it turned out, I always try to make Ronnie's birthday special for him, I never want him to have to wonder if he is worth celebrating or not. I ended up making his favourite, a chocolate mud cake, from scratch, and I carved it into the shape of a three-dimensional dinosaur. It ended up looking really good, he hasn't seen the final product yet, I want it to be a surprise for him tomorrow.

Alice

Tuesday 18 August

Dear Diary,

Today is Ronnie's birthday. He absolutely loved his cake; he didn't want to cut it! I gave him a second guitar, this one an electric one, and he has been playing it all day. He sounds so good when he plays, it is such a delight to listen to him.

Alice

Friday 21 August

Dear Diary,

I finished work just after eight o'clock this morning and went straight home to pack my suitcase in time to catch my plane just after noon. I am so worried about leaving Ronnie with my mother, but it is only for a few days, and he can call me whenever he wants to. I went straight from the airport to the In Vitro Fertilisation clinic and had my screening tests done. Then back to the hotel, where I am currently stretched out on an uber-comfy bed, air conditioning on full blast, watching some reality television. Tomorrow is the reunion; I am already nervous and regretting my decision to come.

Alice

Saturday 22 August

Dear Diary,

As I walked into the reunion, I saw a sea of faces, familiar, albeit older, faces. Each face I recognised was attached to a different, distinct memory, each one as painful and as awkward as the next. Despite my fears, I was not the only one who had turned up alone, and there were many new faces there as well, spouses and children of former classmates. It wasn't the horror evening I was expecting it to be. Christopher was there, my very first crush. Sexy as hell in high school, he was a drummer, and although everyone knew he was dating, it didn't stop half of the population from swooning all over him, myself included. Christopher has not aged well; it is clear that the rock and roll lifestyle took its toll on him. no longer with his childhood sweetheart, he showed up with a date I wrongly mistook for his daughter. It was interesting to see just how all of my bullies have aged and changed since school, not all of them for the better. I am glad that I went, it gave me closure to see everyone, and it put my soul at ease, seeing that not everyone had the life they had wanted and that not everyone was perfectly happy and rich.

Alice

Wednesday 26 August

Dear Diary,

Having spent even the shortest amount of time back in Brisbane City, it has made me ache to move back there, back to civilisation. I should never have allowed my mother to guilt me into moving to Alice Springs for her, it is something that I have regretted every single day since. I think that if I ever intend to meet someone and maybe get married, then I need to be living in a large city, where there are things to do other than hanging out at a pub. Despite everything, I still cannot give up my dream of getting married. Stupid, I know, but still...Maybe one day.

Alice

SEPTEMBER

Wednesday 2 September

Dear Diary,

I hate my job so much, some days I just sit on the edge of my bed and think of ways in which I would injure myself enough so that I need to stay home, but not enough that I would need an operation or hospitalisation. That is pretty bad.

Alice

Thursday 3 September

Dear Diary,

Honestly, the bullying that I have to put up with at work each day is so demoralising. I am always, deliberately, left out. I feel discriminated against by the virtue that I am never included. Not sure if that is real discrimination or not, so I don't say anything. The same way I never used to say anything when my mother and my sister would get up in the morning and get ready for work, carpooling to the train station, returning shortly before dinnertime, laden down with shopping bags and giggles. They would get up and get dressed for work, lying, leaving, as usual, to have a day out together, shopping and lunching, all so that they did not have to tell me what they were doing. I asked once why they didn't just tell me and then they could wear normal clothes instead of their fancy work clothes, and I was told that they didn't tell me as they thought that I would want to go with them. My mother and my sister did everything together, to the point that they even shared a credit card. I suggested once that my mother also get me an additional card, and my mother and my sister both nearly hit the roof, they were so incensed. My mother told me that I could apply for my own if I wanted one. To this day, I have never been on a shopping day, never lunched with anyone. Whenever I see a shopping day portrayed in the movies, I always watch it fascinated, it is so alien to me. I wonder if it is as fun as it looks? What do they talk about all day? I don't imagine that I will ever know. Maybe if I am lucky enough, Ronnie will grow up and get married. Maybe I will have a granddaughter that I could take shopping for the day, that would be nice.

Alice

Friday 4 September

Dear Diary,

I spent the day trawling through the multitude of internet job sites, shortlisting ones that I wanted to apply for. There were quite a few I am going to apply for, I just hope that I can make it to the interview stage. I feel that the older I get, with no qualifications, the less likely I am to be successful. Of course, with no job, I can't get the skills I need to get a job, such a catch twenty-two.

Alice

Tuesday 8 September

Dear Diary,

Another staff morning tea today, this one because an employee I have never heard of before is leaving. My department has a staff morning tea literally every week, for one reason or another. There is always way too much food brought in, the waste is shameful! I no longer contribute anything to the morning teas, and therefore I do not go to them. I used to stress myself out so much, trying to work out what to take, but after being embarrassed one too many times, I just don't bother anymore. Nothing I take in is ever eaten, no matter how nice it is, whenever someone goes to have some, it is pointed out to them that I brought it in, and a secret smile is shared, and the food is placed back on the plate. I even tried bringing in a packet of store-bought biscuits once, not only did the same thing happen, but I got questioned as to why I had only brought in the one packet. I can't afford to waste money or food, and I was always too upset and anxious to eat anything at the morning tea, the room went silent whenever I went to join in anyway. Now I just bake or buy the treat and leave it at home, sending it to school with Ronnie, or taking some to work for myself.

Alice

Wednesday 9 September

Dear Diary,

I am so fed up with my work environment, it has become so toxic. I can't approach management, as living in a small town means that everyone knows everyone else, and my manager and direct supervisor are especially close friends. It has become so bad that no one talks in my office anymore. We all just sit there, in intense, stifling silence, waiting for the phone to ring.

Alice

Thursday 10 September

Dear Diary,

Applied for more jobs today, still no news about any interviews.

Alice

Saturday 12 September

Dear Diary,

I can feel myself sliding into a downward spiral of depression over my work situation. I have lost count of the number of jobs that I have applied for during the past month. When I get home, I have no energy to do anything but to blob on the lounge with Ronnie, I don't even have the oomph to write in my darn diary! So much for sticking to that new year's promise. I am just so tired of everything. Why can't people be nice? Is it really that hard to have a nice working relationship? You don't have to like everyone you work with, but I think you do need to be polite and respectful. Am I the only one who thinks that anymore? Some days I feel as if I am working with a room full of toddlers.

Alice

Wednesday 16 September

Dear Diary,

I am seriously thinking about just quitting my job, even if I don't have a new job lined up to go to yet, it has become that bad for me. Today I found an email on the printer that another staff member had printed out, warning another staff member to be careful what they said around me, and telling them that everything was perfect in that office until I came along and that I effectively ruined everything for the girls there.

Alice

Monday 28 September

Dear Diary,

I made my decision and today I sent my boss an email, mostly as I am a chicken, informing her that I was handing in my resignation, effective in fourteen days, the required amount of time that I am obligated to give. I also lodged another doctor's certificate, giving me another two weeks off work. I have essentially finished up at the office now. I cleaned out my locker before I took my first lot of sick leave, there is no reason for me to set foot in that place again.

Alice

OCTOBER

Friday 2 October

Dear Diary,

I got to the school early to collect Ronnie, and was stunned when I saw Caleb, he looked so gorgeous today, it quite literally took my breath away. It made me sad and wistful all at once.

Alice

Tuesday 6 October

Dear Diary,

Not much happening has been happening in my life lately, I am still looking for work, and still hoping to find my ideal position. I have been walking a lot during the day while Ronnie is at school, doing laps and laps of my garden, front and back. I find it quite soothing actually, and I am even thinking that the next time I go to the local department store, I may try to find where they keep their scales and test them out to see how much I weigh. It will be interesting to see if I have lost any weight or not.

Alice

Friday 9 October

Dear Diary,

Ronnie came home from school today all excited. Caleb has decided to hold a school concert, and all of the music students have been given a part, from every single school that he teaches at. Ronnie has been given an especially hard piece to learn, and he has been practising it ever since we got home.

Alice

Monday 12 October

Dear Diary,

I had a job interview today, which was very exciting. It was with the local council, as an administrative assistant on the front desk, which I think I would be very good at. I have all my fingers and toes crossed.

Alice

Sunday 18 October

Dear Diary,

I took Ronnie to the local night markets tonight. Not for any reason other than to get out of the house and the markets were something a bit different. We rarely go, as every time we do, the sellers are always the same, selling the exact same stuff we can wait eighteen months between visits, and nothing will have changed. It is a nice stroll up and down the mall though, which is where the markets are held. We always run into people we know, tonight we saw one of Ronnie's teachers and her cute puppy, and we also saw Caleb, there performing with his rock band. I was so proud of myself. As much as I wanted to just stop and drool, I just kept walking, I didn't even glance in his direction. I won't embarrass Ronnie again, and I won't allow myself to get my hopes up only to have them crushed. No matter how sexy he looked in his skinny black jeans and band tee-shirt, guitar slung across his shoulder, resting on his hips.

Alice

Friday 23 October

Dear Diary,

Tonight was Ronnie's school concert, and he played so beautifully! It was a joy to watch. As we were leaving, Ronnie took me through a shortcut, through the music room so that he could pick up his jacket. As we were going to go through the door, Caleb was coming out and we nearly collided. Oh gosh, he looked good! He said hello, and I don't know what happened, my brain just stopped. I couldn't talk. I tried to say hello, to wish him a good night, but I couldn't form a coherent sentence. I was a stuttering, mumbling, babbling fool. In the end, I just grabbed Ronnie's hand and rushed past, I was so mortified! I just wanted to die of embarrassment.

Alice

Saturday 24 October

Dear Diary,

I have not been able to stop thinking, and obsessing, over my embarrassing encounter with Caleb yesterday. I should have said something to him. I should have mentioned the concert to him, said thank you for hosting it. I am so ashamed; he must have thought that I was so stupid!

Alice

Monday 26 October

Dear Diary,

I found out today that I got the job at the town council! I am so excited! It seems like a really good fit, with nice, honest, genuine employees, and regular, standard hours of work. I start next week.

Alice

Friday 30 October

Dear Diary,

I saw Caleb when I collected Ronnie from school today, despite my mortification over the school concert night still fresh in my mind, and HE SMILED AT ME! He actually smiled a full, dimpled glory smile. At me. I even looked behind me to see if there was someone else standing there that he could have been smiling at, but no, it was just me. I gave him a small smile back. I have done nothing all afternoon but think about that smile.

Alice

Saturday 31 October

Dear Diary,

I took Ronnie trick or treating tonight. We don't celebrate Halloween in Australia, but Alice Springs has a large number of Americans who come here to work at Pine Gap, a supposed spy base. They tend to all live in the more affluent part of town, and each year they celebrate Halloween. Most of the town goes over there to trick or treat, you are pretty much guaranteed to run into someone that you know. Ronnie decided to go dressed as a Deoxyribonucleic Acid strand, which was a super hard costume for me to have to make. I went as my favourite witch from a family movie featuring three witches, I just adore it! It was a fun night, just me and my main man, wandering the streets until eight o'clock at night, collecting candy and treats. When we got home, we sat up together and watched our favourite

Halloween movie and the inspiration for my costume. Ronnie loves to pretend that he is the ghost boy from the movie, trying to save the little girl kidnapped by the witches.

Alice

NOVEMBER

Monday 2 November

Dear Diary,

I started my new job, and it is fantastic. Honestly, it is such a relief to work there, so refreshing to work in an environment where everybody is respected and valued, such a different work culture from the one that I was used to. I felt so empowered today, just really happy, with my work situation, with life in general, something that has not happened in a long time. When I went to eat lunch today, the staffroom was really busy, and staff made room for me at the table, they welcomed me in, they included me in the conversation, explaining what they had been talking about so that I didn't feel excluded. Just before my lunch break was over, I sent Caleb a quick text message, telling him that I really enjoyed the concert and that it was nice seeing him, that he always brightened my day. And more than that, I actually sent it. I feel good about sending it, I can even actually, genuinely say that if he doesn't text me back, I will be totally okay with that. Well, almost totally okay.

Alice

Thursday 5 November

Dear Diary,

Caleb replied to my text message! I am floating on cloud nine. He texted me to see if I would like to go out for coffee with him. like a date. On a date. With Caleb. Me! I just froze when I saw those words. I couldn't reply, I was so paralysed with giddy excitement. I have never been asked out on a date before. I have never been on a date before. It is all new to me. I texted him back, and said yes, obviously, as if I would ever say anything else.

Alice

Friday 6 November

Dear Diary,

I am having coffee with Caleb tomorrow. Even as I write that it seems surreal! I have never been on a date; I am so nervous. How ridiculous is that? A thirty-five-year-old woman who is about to go on her first date. Gosh, I have never even been flirted with before, let alone been asked out on a date! I just hope that this does not end up being a gigantic disaster!

Alice

Saturday 7 November

Dear Diary,

I could not get to sleep last night, I could not stop thinking about my date tonight, words I never ever thought that I would be able to say. I have so many questions, I wish that I had someone to ask, someone to talk to for advice, but I don't. I have never been kissed, is that something that happens on a first date? Should it be a peck on the cheek, or is that too old fashioned? I just don't know what I should do, what the dating protocol or etiquette is. I mean, does he pay, or do I? Or do we split it, and how the hell does one even bring that question up without sounding rude or nervous? Should I eat properly, like I normally would, or do I just nibble at my food? I looked it up on the internet, and one of the advice columns that I read said to nibble, that women should not act like a pig by eating their full meal, but isn't that a waste of food, not to mention an obvious lie? Who would believe that? Should I laugh at what he says? Even if it isn't very funny? How do I sit? What do I do with my arms? Cross them? Rest them on my lap? What are some interesting questions I can ask Caleb to show that I am interested? I know that I am obsessing over this, too much maybe? Does anyone else go through these thoughts when they get asked out on a date, or is it just me? I don't want to embarrass myself or make Caleb regret asking me out, I just want to get this right.

Alice

Sunday 8 November

Dear Diary,

My first date was not, as I had imagined it would be, a disaster. In fact, it was really rather nice. We went to a local café place in town, a place that I really love, with an easy, relaxed vibe, so there was no pressure to make conversation in dark corners. It was quiet enough to talk but relaxed enough for there to be no pressure. I had such fun. We ended up ordering from their new menu, a variety tasting plate, which was actually really delicious, and coffee. I was so nervous when I left home, but by the time we were at the café, my nerves had settled down. It was a really nice night actually, we just talked, like normal people, without any weirdness or awkwardness, as if we had known each other our entire lives. Will I see him again? I hope so, I am not very forward though, so if he doesn't call me, I probably won't call him, I would be too worried that he was trying to let me down gently and would just leave it as it was.

Alice

Sunday 15 November

Dear Diary,

I have spoken to Caleb every day this week, which in itself feels surreal. I have no idea what is happening, I mean, seriously, I literally have no idea if we are still classed as friends, or if we are now dating, or what we would be labelled. I had no idea that I could feel like this, lighter somehow.

Alice

Monday 16 November

Dear Diary,

If we are in fact dating, then today was our second date. Caleb and I had coffee, at his house, and it was not at all weird. I didn't feel uncomfortable or awkward or anxious at all. I felt rather normal.

Alice

Wednesday 18 November

Dear Diary,

My holiday leave was paid out from my last job, but as I started a new one, I am not actually going away this year. To be honest, with the whole Caleb thing, I am not at all upset by it.

Alice

Friday 20 November

Dear Diary,

Caleb took me to see his band tonight, which was amazing, when we got back to my place, he took my hand and drew me close, and danced with me. He said that he had wanted to do that all night. Major swoon on my behalf. It would be too easy to fall in love, to lose my heart to this man, perhaps I already have?

Alice

Wednesday 25 November

Dear Diary,

I told Caleb about my past tonight. I wasn't going to, but I could feel myself starting to pull away from him, and I wanted him to know why that was happening, and that it really was not a conscious decision. I thought it was best that he knew, upfront, what type of mess he was getting himself into. I think a part of me was thinking that when he found out that he would not want to see me again, it is only a matter of time really, so I got in first and told him, before he had time to break my heart. The funny thing is, he didn't seem to care. Oh, he cared about what had happened, about the impact that it had had on me and my life, but he was not at all put off by it. He just sat there and held my hand while I told him, and then he thanked me for telling him, for being honest. We just sat together, in peaceful, companionable, silence, occasionally kissing, for ages, and when he brought me home tonight, he kissed me, and he told me that he would see me tomorrow. Not once did he make me justify my response to the rape and abuse, not once did he question if my memory was correct. It was refreshing, amazing actually.

Alice

Friday 27 November

Dear Diary,

Caleb invited me to his place for dinner tomorrow, and he assured me that he will be cooking. I have butterflies in my stomach, my nerve endings are all tingly with anticipation. Tomorrow might be the night that I stay over at Caleb's, but I am not putting any pressure on myself, if it happens it happens, if not, well, I am sure there will be other opportunities.

Alice

Sunday 29 November

Dear Diary,

I spent last night at Caleb's house! I feel like I just want to squeal that from the rooftops. As promised, he made us dinner. Afterwards, we just hang out, no pressure, no expectations. He played the guitar for me, a couple of songs he has been writing for an album he is launching soon. He oozes rock star sex appeal, he's irresistible really. As he finished one of his songs, I just couldn't stop myself, I all but launched myself at him, I just had a desperate need to kiss him, however silly that sounds. One thing just led to another really, we were combustible. There were achingly slow caresses mixed with feather touches, fire hot kisses combined with the sweetest of moans. It was my choice. Caleb was my choice, and for that reason alone, it will be a night that I will never forget.

Alice

DECEMBER

Tuesday 1 December

Dear Diary,

Christmas season is my favourite time of the year!
Work is all decked out as festive as can be and wearing
Christmas themed accessories is fully encouraged. I
feel like I am in a dream that I will surely wake from
any day now.

Alice

Wednesday 2 December

Dear Diary,

Caleb sprung me singing today, I was mortified! I was sitting in my office at home, browsing the internet, singing along to the latest hits on the radio, when I became aware that he was standing leaning against the wall, listening, a smile on his sexy face. He told me not to stop, but I was too self-conscious to keep going.

Alice

Monday 7 December

Dear Diary,

I have been wondering if I should invite Caleb for Christmas lunch? I know that he is staying in Alice Springs for Christmas this year, and I know that I will want to see him over Christmas, hopefully, he feels the same way about me.

Alice

Tuesday 8 December

Dear Diary,

I asked Caleb to join us for Christmas lunch, and he said yes, with his cheeky smile that makes his dimples appear and leaves me tingling inside. I am in so much trouble.

Alice

Friday 11 December

Dear Diary,

Today was the last day of term for Ronnie, I was lucky enough to get time off work to go pick him up. The last day of term is special for Ronnie and I. It was nice to have that moment before the craziness of Christmas really kicks in.

Alice

Saturday 12 December

Dear Diary,

One of our favourite days of the year today. Ugly tee-shirt day. Each year Ronnie and I host an ugly tee-shirt making party. Everyone decorates an ugly tee shirt and they then get to keep it. Ronnie and I keep ours and wear them on Christmas day, which is always fun. This year Caleb joined us, and he and Ronnie made matching shirts with Santa playing the guitar, which was adorable!

Alice

Wednesday 16 December

Dear Diary,

I'm not sure if I should buy Caleb a Christmas gift?
Are there rules around this kind of thing?

Alice

Friday 18 December

Dear Diary,

Work had their Christmas lunch today, and as
everyone has been so nice to me since I started, I
thought I would make something to take in. The whole

office actually closes for their lunch, for two hours, so that no one misses out, how cool is that? I made two large gingerbread houses and decorated them to look like the outside of the town council building. They were a huge hit!

Alice

Saturday 19 December

Dear Diary,

Today Ronnie and I had our annual gingerbread house making party. Every year we have the same people over, more or less, and it is always a really busy, noisy, fun affair. I make all of the gingerbread, and then assemble all of the houses, a bit of a necessity as none of the people we invite are bakers and constructing the houses can be a nightmare. Then everyone brings a bag or two of lollies and everyone shares everything. We have had some wild creations through the years, from churches and snowy chalets to log cabins and beach shacks. One year we even had a demolition site as a result of a guest miscalculating the number of lollies her roof could hold! It really is such a fun way to spend a day. Caleb worked today so wasn't able to come, a blessing really, as I was teased non-stop over my romance.

Alice

Sunday 20 December

Dear Diary,

Ronnie and I went Christmas shopping today. I already have all my gifts and stocking stuffers, but it is fun to go out at Christmastime, and Ronnie asked if he could get a couple of things. Ronnie doesn't know it, but I have gotten him a video game console for Christmas and my mother has purchased him a couple of games to go with it. I cannot wait to see his face on Christmas morning, he has wanted this console for so long.

Alice

Thursday 24 December

Dear Diary,

I love Christmas eve; it is usually a mostly peaceful day for us. My mother always eats too much and then naps all afternoon, which is nice for Ronnie and I. Caleb came over this afternoon, and we played a game that is a tradition in my house, twelve days of Christmas. It is pretty simple, we merely write our own lyrics to the song of the same name, and then we read them out to each other. It is always really interesting to see what everyone else has put down. Sometimes people theme their lists, other times they are realistic, or plain fantasy, either way, they are always funny. This year Ronnie themed his list around his favourite British spy, and mine was a bit more realistic.

My list:

One inground swimming pool.

Two massaged feet.

Three more cake pans.

Four weeks at the beach.

Five new pieces of Christmas crockery.

Six more lost kilos.

Seven years subscription to a stationery box.

Eight pretty summer dresses.

Nine months traipsing the world.

Ten more fruit trees planted out the back.

Eleven new bath sheets.

Twelve million dollars (okay, so not totally realistic).

Actually, I can cross off number two, Caleb took care of that for me before he went home. I thought about asking him to stay the night here, seeing as he is coming over tomorrow anyway, but I don't think I am ready for him to have to face my household first thing in the morning, I would rather not scare him off just yet!

Alice

Friday 25 December

Dear Diary,

Christmas day lunch was one of the nicest I have ever had. My mother managed to behave herself all the way through until the dessert was served, at which point she could not help but utter a criticism, over the fact that I had only purchased her a small fruit cake this year, instead of a large one. Caleb, on his second miniature caramel pie, replied without batting an eyelid, telling her that buying a large one would have been wasteful as she is the only one who eats fruit cake. Oh. My. Goodness! No one has ever stuck up for me before, I was dumbstruck. As I expected, Ronnie's gift was a huge hit, as was the gift that Caleb bought for me, a custom made, traditionally hammered, metal ring inscribed with the word FIERCE. He gave it to me in private and told me that this was how he saw me, and he wanted to make sure that I never forgot it. in the end, I decided not to buy Caleb a gift, instead, I made him one. I rented a microphone from the local music shop and recorded myself singing, for Caleb, just a single song, a favourite of mine that I recently discovered he also loved. His smile when he opened it was worth all of the angst and nerves that I had felt beforehand.

Alice

Tuesday 29 December

Dear Diary,

This year was probably the most interesting and bizarre of my life. I honestly cannot believe that I was brave enough to write down a large portion of the abuse that I suffered as a child, or that I was able to write about the trauma of my childhood rape. Somehow, just by writing these down, I feel more powerful, as if I have released it out into the universe and am now on the path of healing and maybe even one day, acceptance, of myself as I am, instead of mourning for the person that I was, that I should have been. Altogether this year I lost twenty-three kilos, which I know does not sound like much, but for me is a huge achievement. A took a crazy, stupid chance on Caleb, and to my delight found out that he actually liked me. Me. Crazy, fat, ugly, baggage carrying me. I have never had that, never felt that before. At times it has been overwhelming. I feel a sense of peace starting to creep in from the edges of my battered soul, for the first time in twenty-three years, I feel that I can now breathe properly.

Alice

Thursday 31 December

Dear Diary,

What does next year hold? I really don't know. I know that I still hope to take Ronnie on a holiday, maybe to a beach or to the snow. My resolutions for this year were important to me, but for next year, I have pared them down to what I consider to be the most important for me right now.

I Will Not...

- Eat when feeling sad, anxious, worried, lonely or down in the dumps.

- Get annoyed with interfering yet (supposedly) well-meaning relatives.
- Obsess (too much) over past mistakes.
- Keep fantasising about Caleb. I will instead, tell him exactly what it is that I want.

I Will...
- Lose weight and start toning up my muscles.
- Reduce my swearing to an acceptable level.
- Be assertive and more confident.
- Stop apologising for who I am.

Alice

The End

Sample: THE SURGEON'S BABY

The door to the clinic burst open, a frantic Emma rushing through to the reception desk, her heart leaping in her throat, her pulse racing with panic. A problem, how can there be a problem? She was told everything was fine, that the procedure had gone to plan, she was flying home tomorrow!

"Emma, Doctor Delaney is expecting you, go straight through," the receptionist waved her hand vaguely in the direction of a hallway and turned back to her magazine. Emma tried to slow her steps, tried to force down the bile she could taste in the back of her mouth.

"Emma dear, come in," Doctor Delaney places a hand on Emma's back and ushers her through the doorway. "Can I get you anything? Tea? Water?"

"Thank you, I'm-" Emma stops mid-sentence as her eyes land on a second person, paused, framed in the doorway.

"Ah," Doctor Delaney follows Emma's gaze, clapping his hands together. "Ivan, come in, take a seat. Emma, this is Doctor Ivan Delgado, Ivan, this is Emma Roberts," he introduces nervously.

Emma's breath caught in her throat as she tried not to stare at Ivan. "Hi" Emma squeaks, her throat like sandpaper, voice wobbling, betraying her nerves.

"I know you must be worried Emma," Doctor Delaney smiles kindly at her, "and I apologise for being cryptic over the telephone, but I felt it was better to have this discussion in private, with all parties concerned." Emma gave herself a mental shake, and leant forward, nodding. "As you know, you requested insemination using an anonymous donor." Doctor Delaney perused her file on the desk in front of him. "I'm very sorry Emma, I'm not sure how to tell you this, but there was a terrible error in our laboratory, our technicians have somehow mixed up the samples. Instead of the anonymous donor you selected, you were mistakenly inseminated with a sample from a private donor, which was meant for storage only."

"I see." Emma's mind raced. What did he mean, a private donor? It was not really that bad, was it? "While I appreciate you telling me this as soon as you became aware of the error, it really makes no difference to me where the sample came from," Emma shrugs, trying to keep calm. "Unless the private donor has a hereditary medical condition, it doesn't change anything."

"Actually," drawls Ivan, leaning back in his chair and crossing his arms over his broad chest, "it changes everything."

"I don't understand, do you work in the lab?" Emma frowned in confusion, turning away from Ivan to face Doctor Delaney. "What exactly are you saying? Is there something wrong with the sample?" Emma was not sure she could stand to find out, the cost of this first procedure had eaten up all of her savings, if it didn't work...Well, she was not sure when, or even if, she would be able to cobble together enough funds to have another attempt.

"No, the sample is medically viable," Doctor Delaney shuffles the paperwork in Emma's file with a pointed look in Ivan's direction, "but it is complicated."

"He means," Ivan interjects dryly, fixing Emma with a scathing look, "that you are having my baby."

"You can't be serious." Emma felt the colour drain from her face as she sat looking from Doctor Delaney to Doctor Delgado and back again, her mouth gaping open.

"I have never been more serious in my life," Ivan's eyes narrow as he watches Emma fidget in her chair. "If you are pregnant, you will be carrying my child, and I expect to be involved every step of the way. Amicably or court-appointed," Ivan shrugged, "I don't care. No child of mine will grow up without their father." The warning in Ivan's voice was clear, and it sent shivers down Emma's spine.

"Emma," Doctor Delaney reaches forward to pat her hand, "it is too early for us to know, but if you are pregnant, Ivan will not only be the father of your baby, but as the two of you have no contract in place, Ivan will have full legal rights to this baby."

End Of Sample

About The Author

An international bestselling and award-winning author of sweet contemporary romance, Kathleen's novels showcase thought-provoking plots and strong emotions that have been likened to a Hallmark movie. Featuring feisty heroines and strong heroes, where everyone gets a happily ever after. To discover more about Kathleen: Connect on social media

Read More of Kathleen's Books

The Flying Doctor's Christmas Wish
The Brooding Doctor's Christmas Wish
Christmas Wish Collection
The Surgeon's Baby
Fling With The Flying Doctor
The Marriage Deal
Caleb's Song
Cinnamon Kisses and Gingerbread Wishes